Love Comes in Many Shapes
Alice Renaud

The Grand Mar Hotel was already buzzing by the time Bryony stepped through the glass doors into the lobby. The air-conditioned interior was a blessed respite after the oven-dry heat outside.

"Good crowd tonight!" Macie, the receptionist, said as Bryony tapped her name and time of arrival into the registration screen. "Lots of families."

"They're the best," Bryony agreed, surveying the tourists who were already streaming through the doors to the main theatre. She loved interacting with the kids. They were always so excited to see a mermaid.

Maia wasn't in the lobby, but punctuality wasn't one of her many strengths. Bryony glanced towards the doors. Perhaps she'd arrive just before the show started.

Macie seemed to divine what she was thinking. "Aw, don't worry. Your girl is already here, sitting in the front row with an ice lolly. I saw her just before I started my shift ten minutes ago."

A globe of warmth expanded in Bryony's chest. Every day she wondered if Maia would come, and every day, without fault, Maia turned up. In the six months they'd lived together in Las Vegas, she must have seen the show close to three hundred times, but she never seemed to get bored. "I love to see you swim, in your real shape," she'd whispered only the night before when they were snuggled up in bed together.

"I'd better go get changed!" Bryony hurried towards the door that led backstage.

Unlike the other mermaids, she had her own changing room. She'd insisted on it as part of her contract with the hotel. It was little more than a broom cupboard, but she could close the door, and that was all that mattered. No one could see her change into her aquatic shape. No one could discover that, unlike the girls in swimsuits giggling outside, she was the real deal. A shape-shifting mermaid from the Morvann Islands in Wales.

She checked the clock on the wall. Twenty-five minutes to go. Damn, she'd cut it a bit fine. She kicked off her sandals and peeled off her shorts and T-shirt. Her skin was darkening, turning a pearly grey, and thickening. She wiggled her fingers and toes as if that would make the webs grow faster. She wished there was a way to accelerate the shifting process. Perhaps she'd ask Maia to do some research. One of the books of spells she'd brought from London might contain the answer.

A rap on the door. "Ten minutes!" the stage manager called out.

"Coming!" At last, Bryony could feel her tail pushing through her buttocks. Her curly brown hair retracted into her skull. Her nose was flattening, leaving only a single nostril that she could close at will.

Finally, she was ready.

She opened the door. The other mermaids were already lining up, shuffling forward on their fake fishtails. Bryony padded along the corridor on her webbed feet to join the back of the queue.

"Off you go, ladies." The stage manager lifted the black curtain, revealing the ladder that climbed the side of the tank. The lights were dimmed, to hide their entrance. One by one the fake mermaids shimmered up the rungs of metal and dived into the aquarium. Oohs and aahs rose from the invisible audience in the theatre.

Bryony grabbed the ladder and made her ascent, a lot slower than her colleagues. Webbed hands and feet were not designed for climbing. At last, she made it to the top and plunged headlong into the cool water.

The lights brightened. A stunned silence greeted her. She was used to it. She didn't match most people's idea of a mermaid. She swam to the bottom of the aquarium and pressed her face to the glass.

The vast room was full of people, lined up on the rows of seats, or around tables in the bar area. And Maia sat in the front row, less than a yard away. A huge smile lit up her lovely face and her blue eyes sparkled. "Now that's the best mermaid I've ever seen!" she said in a loud voice.

She did this every night. "We French call it *la claque, ma cherie,*" she'd said. "Friends, posing as theatregoers, who clap and cheer to encourage the rest of the audience."

The warm glow in Bryony's chest spread through her limbs. Maia always had her back. She was lover, best friend, and cheerleader rolled

Rainbow Desire

Alice Renaud
Callie Carmen
Gibby Campbell
Patricia Elliott
Viola Russell
Annabel Allan
Estelle Pettersen

ISBN 978-1-914301-17-9

Published 2021
Published by Black Velvet Seductions Publishing

Rainbow Desire Copyright 2021 Alice Renaud, Callie Carmen, Gibby Campbell, Patricia Elliott, Viola Russell, Annabel Allan, Estelle Pettersen
Cover design Copyright 2021 Jessica Greeley

Introduction

When a group of BVS authors suggested the idea of an LGBTQ+ anthology, I was delighted. BVS has always embraced romance and love in all its myriad shades and hues. When the stories came in, I was delighted to find the breadth of stories submitted. I hope you will agree that this is an eclectic collection of short stories exploring the topic of LGBTQ+ love. The collection is as diverse as the authors writing them. As a reader, I have always enjoyed reading anthologies, it is a great way of being introduced to the work of new writers and from the writer's point of view it is a great way of experimenting with a new genre.

The stories within these pages mix soft and tender, often moving and thought provoking, to sexier raunchy pieces. I hope you will enjoy reading them as much as I have.

Richard Savage

CEO, Black Velvet Seductions

into one. "My girl," Bryony whistled in the language of the merfolk, and blew her a kiss.

"The lady's right," a little girl piped. "That's a real mermaid!" And she ran forward to press her face against the glass. Bryony grinned at the child. "*La vérité sort de la bouche des enfants*," Maia often said. Truth comes out of children's mouths.

Other children were getting up and crowding around the aquarium, pointing and shouting with excitement. For the next fifteen minutes, Bryony and the other mermaids cavorted with the fishes, swimming in and out of the bright corals. Time flew by as in a dream. All too soon, they were swimming back to the ladder. The lights dimmed, and the show was over for another day.

When Bryony came out of her dressing room, fully human and dressed, Maia was waiting for her. She threw her arms around her and planted a kiss on her mouth. Happiness bubbled in Bryony's veins like champagne. She loved that Maia was so demonstrative. The public displays of affection hadn't gone down well in the conservative Morvann Islands, but here in Las Vegas they didn't have to hide their love.

Maia snaked an arm around her waist and steered her towards the bar and restaurant area. "Come on. I'm dying for a burger."

The restaurant looked full, but the waitress found them a table in the corner. "Two burgers with all the works, a frozen margarita, and a porn star martini," Maia rattled off.

"You're supposed to call them passion fruit martinis these days." Bryony glanced at the waitress to see if she was offended, but she only laughed. "A lot of folk still call them porn stars. That's OK. My mum used to be one!"

Maia and Bryony were still giggling when their food and drinks arrived. "Only in Vegas," Bryony said.

"Only in Vegas… though I hear LA is the same," Maia laughed, and clinked her glass against Bryony's. "I thought of doing a little flutter on the roulette, but the casino manager looks like he's going to faint every time he sees me. I'll spare the poor man the stress tonight."

Bryony sipped her cocktail, savouring the fruity taste. "No wonder. Your big win six months ago almost bankrupted them. We were barely off the plane, and suddenly we were rich!"

She grinned at the memory. After their hurried departure from Britain, the long flight and the jet lag, it felt as though the Goddess and the Lady of the Sea were scooping them up and hugging them like favoured daughters. It was proof that they'd been right to leave their old lives behind. The win had paid for their beautiful house in a safe, pleasant area of Las Vegas, with a huge garden and an Olympic-sized swimming pool. They'd invested the remainder of the money. The revenue from the investments, added to Bryony's wages and Maia's earnings as a tarot card reader, enabled them to live very comfortably.

"Fortune smiled on us, for sure." Maia licked the rim of sugar on her glass. The sight of her pink tongue sent a sudden arrow of desire into Bryony's belly.

Maia winked at her as if she divined what she was thinking. "Eat up now, your dinner will get cold. Then we can go back home and have some fun!"

By the time they walked out of the hotel into the sparkly Las Vegas night, Bryony was abuzz with anticipation. She stood on the edge of the sidewalk and hailed a taxi. Their house was only twenty minutes away on foot, but that was twenty minutes too much.

A man bumped into her. "Sorry, ma'am." He had an English accent, which made Bryony look at him. The man smiled, revealing perfect white teeth in a bronzed, aristocratic face. He was so handsome that Bryony froze on the spot and gaped at him. He had to be a movie star. The man nodded at her and moved on.

A taxi screeched to a halt. Maia ran up to her. "Hey, who was that? He had his back to me and I didn't see his face. You look stunned!"

Bryony opened the door for her and followed her into the taxi. "I don't know who he was, but he was drop-dead gorgeous. Maybe he's one of these up-and-coming Asian actors from Britain."

"Ooh, I hope so." Maia winked at her. "A gorgeous British man would be just the ticket."

A tendril of disquiet snaked through Bryony's mind. Maia had never expressed an interest in men in front of her, but she knew that she'd had male lovers back in Britain, including the warlock who had taught her magic.

"Do you ever miss men?" She kept her tone casual, but worry extended its tentacles into her throat.

Maia shook her head. "No. But..." her lips curled in a suggestive smile. "Do you ever wonder what it's like, with a man?"

Worry dissolved into sensual heat. Was Maia really suggesting what

Bryony thought she was suggesting?

"Sometimes," Bryony whispered. Maia was her first and only lover. But she'd seen mermen chase their mates across the kelp forest, their members erect and proud... and she'd seen the mermaids giggle, breathless, and pull their mermen by the hand, eager for what they could give them. Sometimes, Bryony did wonder...

Maia winked. "One night, we could pick a man together," she murmured. "One we both like. And bring him back home."

Her words sent a rush of blood to Bryony's loins. "You dirty girl."

Maia poked her tongue at her. "You love it."

The taxi stopped. Bryony paid him and took Maia by the hand. They ran across the manicured lawn, past the swimming pool, and into their house. Bryony flicked the light switch. She wanted to see Maia tonight. All of Maia.

Her girlfriend walked to the dining area and perched on the edge of a chair by the breakfast counter. Her short black skirt rode up her creamy thighs. A tingle started at the base of Bryony's spine. Maia's red lips parted in a sultry smile. "Baby... you look lovely tonight."

A happy flame leaped in Bryony's heart. After six months of living together, Maia's compliments still felt like a miracle. That a woman like Maia, so beautiful, so clever, so talented, should want her and choose to be with her... only her. Bryony still found it hard to believe at times.

"You too," Bryony whispered. She wanted to say more. She wanted to tell Maia how gorgeous she was... a goddess come to earth. She wanted to tell her how much she meant to her. But the words expired on her lips and her throat went dry, because Maia was unbuttoning her blouse.

Bryony's gaze glued itself to the triangle of tanned skin at the base of Maia's throat, a triangle that soon grew longer, and deeper, revealing a pretty green bra that Bryony hadn't seen before. Maia had bought new underwear! The tingle between her legs grew into an itch, and her blood rushed to her head, making her dizzy. All her senses stretched towards Maia... the swell of her breasts above the green lace... her long, shapely legs... the pink tongue that peeped at the corner of her mouth, a sure sign that she was excited. But Bryony held herself in check, resisting the urge to pounce on her girlfriend and ravish her there and then. The delicious anticipation was part of the game, a game she'd never tire of playing.

But Maia had other ideas tonight. Her fingers flew over the

remaining buttons of her blouse, and she yanked it off her shoulders, throwing it carelessly on the floor. Her skirt went the same way, and now she sat there in only her lacy green bra and adorable matching panties. The itch between Bryony's thighs flared into an ache. Her whole body yearned for Maia. She couldn't wait any longer. She closed the distance between them and cupped her shoulders. "You drive me wild, woman."

Maia tilted her head, offering her luscious mouth. "You love it. You—"

Bryony's lips captured hers, silencing her. Maia tasted of lemons and frozen margaritas, the very essence of pleasure. Bryony drank deep, pushing her tongue into her lover's mouth. Her hands glided down to seize Maia's breasts. She massaged them, brushing her thumbs against the hard nipples that poked through the lace. Maia made a little mewing sound in her throat and parted her legs. The scent of her arousal hit Bryony's nostrils, sending her libido into overdrive. Tonight there would be no tender, feathery kisses, no gentle petting. Tonight was a night for mating.

She slid her hand down, under the waistband of Maia's panties. She was wet for her, so wet. The pressure in Bryony's belly increased until she almost moaned aloud. She had to taste her… eat her… devour her. She dropped to her knees and yanked the sodden panties down. Maia arched her back, offering her pussy to Bryony's mouth. "Oh please, baby… Yes, please…"

Bryony pressed her lips to Maia's mound, gratified to feel the deep shudder that ran through her lover. She'd never tire of pleasuring her. She licked the swollen clit, up and down, and round and round. Maia whimpered and dug her fingers in Bryony's hair. A stream of words issued from her mouth, in a language Bryony didn't understand.

But she knew what they meant. Anticipation tightened in her belly. Maia in turn was giving her a gift. The gift of magic. She plunged her tongue into Maia's opening, revelling in the sweet-and-salty taste of her. Maia's incantation rose, high and urgent. Her hands traced a pattern on Bryony's hair.

An unseen force slid between Bryony's thighs from behind, parting them with a speed and strength that made her gasp. She pressed her mouth harder against Maia's pussy and gripped the edges of the chair, trembling with excitement. Maia had divined that she too wanted it rough and fast tonight. And she was giving it to her.

Something invisible, long and hard pushed aside Bryony's panties, and a round head teased her opening. Hot cream spilled to welcome the sweet invasion. It entered her, filling her up, pressing against her cervix, until Bryony felt that she would burst. It was so hard, so good… and now it was moving inside her, slowly at first, then faster. The delicious friction pushed her closer and closer to ecstasy. Maia's juices filled her mouth and her cries filled her ears. "Yes, Bryony, baby, yes, I want us to come together, don't stop, please, don't stop…"

Bryony groaned as the invisible rod inside her pumped harder. Her walls rippled around it, and waves of pleasure drenched her. She tongued Maia and sucked her clit, rasping her teeth against the throbbing flesh. Maia yelped like a vixen and pulled at Bryony's hair. "Baby, yes, yes, yes!"

And she came, convulsing against Bryony's mouth, her release gushing out of her in a sweet stream of liquid. Maia's ecstasy added fuel to the furnace burning in Bryony's loins. Maia's magic pulsed in her veins, filling her with liquid fire. She was melting… burning… she couldn't take any more… She threw her head back and howled as the wild orgasm ripped through her, tearing her to shreds and scattering her across the stars.

When she came to her senses, the invisible force had left her. But the magic was still there. Because Maia was holding her, kissing her hair, murmuring in her ear. "Baby, you make me feel so good."

Bryony struggled to her feet, her legs wobbly with pleasure, and helped Maia up. "Let's go take a shower."

They washed and dried each other, then curled up in bed, naked in each other's arms. Bryony closed her eyes. Another perfect evening.

Maia nuzzled her neck. "I love trying out new spells on you."

"Hmm." Bryony stifled a yawn. "I love your spells."

"If we were in London, I'd ask my ex-master for some new tricks, to stretch my repertoire a bit." A wistful note had crept into Maia's voice. Unease seeped into Bryony's mind, tainting her contentment. She often worried that Maia might be getting bored with Vegas… bored with a life among ordinary humans.

Bored with her.

The fear was always there, lurking at the bottom of Bryony's soul. Wide awake now, she rolled to face her girlfriend. Tonight, she wouldn't remain silent. She'd take the bull by the horns. If Maia was unhappy, she had to know, and try to fix it.

"Do you miss London? The life you used to have?"

Maia hugged her tighter. "Baby, I'm happy. Don't ever, for one second, think that I regret coming here with you. These past six months have been the best of my life."

She sounded sincere, but the note of wistfulness still vibrated under the tender words. Bryony stroked her lover's back and dared to probe a little more. "But you sometimes wish that you could see your friends again? The witches and warlocks you used to work with?"

Maia sighed. "Sometimes. Some of them. They were my whole life for five years. And I learned a lot from them. Especially from Ariel."

Ariel. The name fell between them like a stone. Bryony's stomach tightened around a hard ball of disquiet. Maia didn't often talk about the powerful warlock who had been her master, and her lover. He had taught her all the magic she knew, including the sensual spells that Bryony enjoyed so much. Ariel, the leader of the warlocks and witches of London, the most renowned sorcerer in Britain, the handsome, charming man that very few women could resist. Bryony couldn't compete with him.

She knew she should have kept quiet. Let Maia go to sleep. Why stir up trouble? But she couldn't stop herself from probing the painful spot.

"Perhaps he will come to visit."

Maia stiffened, then let out a forced laugh. "Oh, by the Goddess, Ariel would never leave Britain! He's way too scared that someone would take his place in his absence, or that the hags would launch an attack. No, he'll never set foot in the US. And a good thing too. We didn't part on good terms. He didn't want me to leave."

She kissed Bryony's brow. "I'm happy with you here, baby. I don't need anyone else."

Bryony rested her head on Maia's shoulder. "I'm glad."

Soon Maia's even breath told Bryony that she'd fallen asleep. But she lay awake for a long time, staring at the darkness. Something in Maia's voice had troubled her.

When Bryony had suggested that Ariel might one day come to Vegas, Maia had sounded afraid. Why? From what Bryony had heard of Ariel, he'd never hurt a woman just because she'd left him. So why would Maia fear his visit so muchBryony had always had the nagging suspicion that her lover had not told her the whole truth about her past life. Maia had said that she'd been tired of London, that she'd wanted a fresh start, and that was why she'd come to Wales. To the Morvann

Islands, Bryony's homeland. But Bryony had suspected there was more to it than that. Now her suspicions were hardening into certainty. How could she convince Maia to open up?

She fell asleep without having found an answer.

***

The next morning, her wallet had disappeared. "Oh, drat." Bryony let out a groan as she searched the living room for the tenth time. "I must have dropped it in the restaurant, or perhaps in the taxi."

"Would you like me to try a finding spell?" Maia traced a figure in the air. Bryony shook her head. "No, don't worry, you'll be late for your tarot session. I only had twenty dollars in there. Good thing I didn't take my credit card yesterday."

"If you're sure." Maia grabbed her by the waist and planted a kiss on her lips. "I'll be back early afternoon."

She had a few private clients in Las Vegas, for whom she read tarot cards and tea leaves. This morning's customer lived in an exclusive gated property on the other side of town. She was an old lady who enjoyed Maia's company as much as her divination skills, and always insisted on treating her to lunch.

"Have fun!" Bryony waved her girlfriend goodbye and headed for the pool.

The water sparkled, blue and inviting under the cloudless sky, a giant sapphire framed by the green velvet of the lawn. Bryony peeled off her clothes, put her phone down on top of her T-shirt, and plunged into the cool water.

She loved their pool. It was perfectly secluded, surrounded by trees and bushes that hid her from prying eyes. Bryony dived to the bottom and began to shift. Twenty minutes later, she emerged in full mermaid shape, to discover that her phone was ringing. She reached out a webbed hand and grabbed it. "Hello?"

"Hello, is this Bryony Benetynn?" The voice was male, educated, and British.

"Yes, it is!" Bryony usually hated cold callers, but she was in a good mood this morning and didn't want to be unpleasant to a fellow Brit.

"Miss Benetynn, I have your wallet. I found it on the pavement yesterday evening after I bumped into you. You must have dropped it just before you got into the taxi."

Oh My Dizzy Aunt. It was the British hunk from last night. Little sparks of excitement danced in Bryony's chest.

"I found your card with your number and address in your wallet." The soft baritone glided into her ears like hot honey. "I was passing by and thought I might hand it back to you? I'm standing outside the gates right now."

The little sparks grew brighter and spread into Bryony's belly. It wasn't every day you got to meet a movie star. "Can you give me fifteen minutes to dry and get dressed? I'm in the pool, you see. Then I'll come to the gate to let you in."

"Oh, there's no need to trouble yourself," the smooth voice said, right behind her.

Bryony wheeled round, too shocked to speak. The man from yesterday was standing on the other side of the pool, smiling.

And she was in full aquatic shape.

"How the hell did you get in?" She hoped that the irritation she put in her voice would disguise her fear.

The man inclined his head to the side, studying her as if she were an interesting wild animal. "Locks and keys aren't usually a problem for me."

He was a burglar! Or worse! Bryony fought the rising tide of panic and fumbled with her phone to call the police. It slipped from her wet hands and fell into the water. She let out a cry of distress.

"Bryony, please, don't be scared. I'm not a thief or a murderer, and I'm not going to hurt you. I just want to talk to you." The intruder's voice had a soothing, almost sing-song quality, and Bryony, to her surprise, found that her fear was receding. The man was telling the truth. He meant her no harm.

Then she wondered why she believed him so easily.

"Can you look away? I'm going to change out of my mermaid costume. I was practising for my show at the Grand Mar Hotel, you see."

"Great show. I saw it yesterday." The man's black eyes held hers, and she had the uneasy feeling that he could see right into her mind. "But you don't need to worry. I know all about your people, and you're not the first mermaid I've seen in her aquatic shape." He gave her a dazzling smile. "My name is Ariel Wolfsbane, and I'm a warlock."

A dark pit opened up in Bryony's stomach. She should have guessed. That was why he had got in so easily, and why he had charmed her so fast. She wondered if he had put a spell on her.

"Are you using magic on me?" Damn, her tone was more challenging than was wise, but he was scaring her, and she didn't like to be scared. She'd never met a warlock before, but she'd heard many tales of their powers. Some sorcerers were good, some not so much, and she didn't know which category this Wolfsbane fitted into. Plus, there was his history with Maia. Hot, acidic jealousy surged, and mingled with her fear to produce anger. "You'd better not be using any of your enchantments, because—"

Because what? From what Maia had said, he was the most powerful wizard in Britain, so she had no chance against him.

He presented his hands to her, palms upwards, as if to say *Look, no tricks.* "I promise I'm not casting any spells right now. I am hoping we can resolve this… situation… peacefully. I am a friend of the merfolk, and I have no wish to pick a fight with a mermaid, even one so far from home." His tone grew even softer. "Also, I haven't come to take your girlfriend from you. I just want to talk."

The toxic mix of anguish and anger inside Bryony's chest receded a little. He really didn't seem to mean her harm. And at least she didn't have to worry about him seeing her in her aquatic shape. Warlocks and witches were not like ordinary humans; they knew about the merfolk. If he was no threat to her or her relationship, perhaps she could afford to be polite—and invite him in. She took a deep breath to calm her nerves.

"OK, we can talk. But you'd better come inside before a human sees me."

"Thank you, Bryony." He bowed, an old-fashioned gesture in a relatively young man, but it suited him somehow.

She plunged to the bottom of the pool to retrieve her phone, then scrambled out of the water and grabbed her clothes. "After you." She didn't want him to follow her. She wanted him where she could see him.

He walked up the path towards the house in long, easy strides. In spite of her unease, Bryony couldn't help noticing his long, lean legs encased in dark jeans, and his ass—the most perfect ass she'd ever seen on a man. Even from the back, it was enough to distract any woman—or mermaid. Enough to make her libido whisper that whatever he might want, she was minded to give it to him.

Guilt stabbed her, sharp and sudden, yanking her back to reality. What the hell was she doing fantasizing about this guy that she'd only just met? A dangerous warlock who had broken into her property. What would Maia think?

Maia! She had to protect her. She had to get rid of Ariel before her lover got back.

She sped through the lawn after him and into the house.

The cool air inside was like a balm, and he let out a sigh. "How lovely to be out of the sun. I can't believe it's already so hot outside. It's not even late morning."

His ordinary words soothed Bryony a little. Perhaps it would be all right. Perhaps he'd only come to say hello and find out how Maia was.

Yeah, right. The chief warlock of London would totally cross the Atlantic just to have a chat. Not. She forced herself to keep her tone light. "We Brits struggle a bit in this climate. It'll be worse in July." She waved him into the vast living room. "Make yourself comfortable. I'll get changed and come back as soon as I can."

Ariel settled on the white leather sofa and gave her a mesmerizing smile. "Don't rush on my account. We have plenty of time."

She wished he would stop using his charm on her. It made her go soft and gooey inside, when she wanted to keep her wits about her. With his looks and glamour, he didn't even need magic to cast a spell on women. Females of every species probably fell at his feet all the time. She was beginning to wonder how Maia could ever have left him. Perhaps he would tell her.

"I'll be fifteen minutes tops," she promised and hurried out of the room. Perhaps Ariel's sudden arrival was an opportunity rather than a threat. A chance for her to learn the truth about Maia's sudden departure from London.

She scooted up the stairs as fast as she could on her webbed feet and dashed into the master bedroom. She didn't like to leave the warlock to his own devices in her house, but she'd no choice. She had to get back into human shape, and she couldn't be naked in front of him.

Though *he* might like it, a little devil in the corner of her mind whispered. And perhaps she would like him to look at her. Bryony gritted her teeth and threw open the closet that contained her clothes. She had never, ever dreamed of being unfaithful to Maia, so why did these crazy ideas keep popping into her head? She dug her toes into the thick purple carpet, impatient for the webs to recede. Her hair was reappearing on her head, and she pulled at it to make it grow faster. Sure, Maia had hinted that one day they might pick a man up and bring him home to have their wicked way with him, but Maia sure as hell hadn't had this man in mind. It would be like inviting a tiger in for tea, like in the book that she used to love as a child. A beautiful, sinuous, sexy tiger…

She groaned at herself and dragged her hands through her hair, as if to dislodge the inappropriate thought. There *was* something cat-like about Ariel, in the silent grace of his movements and his bright, watchful eyes.

Butterflies tap-danced down her spine. Of disquiet or excitement, she didn't know anymore. With a start she realised that she wanted to feel Ariel's eyes on her… and she wanted him to like what he saw. Her hand hovered over her dresses and selected a sparkly, midnight-blue chiffon number. It was one of her favorites, because it made her pale skin gleam like ivory, and gave her blue eyes a deeper shade, a hint of sapphire.

She took it off the hanger and let it glide over her head. It clung to her small breasts, flared over her hips, and fell in glittery folds just above her knees. She glanced at herself in the mirror. Perfect. She slid her feet into strappy sandals but didn't bother with underwear. Like most merfolk, she usually went commando, as bras and panties were a hindrance when shifting.

She wasn't doing anything wrong, she told herself as she sashayed down the stairs. If she looked good, she'd feel more confident, and the conversation with Ariel would be easier if he found her attractive. Besides, if Maia came back early, she wanted to look her best next to the man who had been her lover.

She wondered if Ariel would have taken advantage of her absence to wander around the house, but no, he was sitting exactly where she'd left him, his long legs stretched in front of him. He looked up when she entered, and a slow, sexy smile of appreciation spread over his lips. "You look even more ravishing than last night. This is a lovely dress, and it fits you like a dream."

The flattery sent a shiver of pleasure through her. She had no idea why she craved his compliments so much. She'd never felt that way before, except with Maia.

His gaze glided over her like a caress, and her body responded with a strength that shocked her. Her knees grew weak, her nipples tightened, and when his eyes lingered on her chest, she knew he could see them poking through the flimsy material.

This was wrong. She should have turned around and run away. But her body didn't obey her. It remained rooted to the spot, basking in his attention… asking for more.

He patted the sofa next to him. "Come and sit here."

Hell, he was giving her orders. In her own house. She knew she should have reacted with indignation, but somehow she couldn't muster the strength. Her body had no intention of resisting this man. Her body wanted to obey him. In everything.

She moved towards him as if in a trance. A vestige of sanity made her perch at the end of the sofa, but it wasn't a very long sofa, so she was still close to him. Close enough to inhale his scent. Something tasteful and expensive, which somehow managed to evoke both an oriental palace and a woodland glade.

It made her mouth water.

He stretched an arm along the back of the sofa, which brought his strong, fine hand a mere inch or two from her head. He'd only have to move his fingers a fraction to touch her dark curls.

Those same fingers had caressed every inch of Maia's body, as Ariel had taught her the sensual magic that Bryony enjoyed so much. The tender spot between her legs tingled at the memory of what they'd done last night. Yes, she should be thankful to Ariel for teaching her lover so well. Who knew what he could do to her, with this magic of his?

A tiny corner of her brain that had remained rational managed to make itself heard. What the fuck was she doing?

She folded her hands on her lap as if they might escape her control and creep towards him. "What did you want to talk to me about?"

He withdrew his arm. Bryony couldn't help a twinge of regret. His beautiful face grew serious. "Your family send their regards."

Guilt surged, dissipating the seductive haze he'd woven around her. Over the past six months, she'd tried not to think too much about the folk she'd left behind. Now every worry she'd pushed away flooded her mind. "How are they? Are they OK? Are they very angry with me?"

Ariel's smile had a different quality this time. It was full of understanding, compassion even, and damn it, it made him even hotter. Dark, dangerous, charismatic… and kind? She had no chance.

"They're all well. And no, they're not angry with you, Bryony. Not any more. They're just worried. I told them that if I found you, I'd give them news of you. Is that all right?"

Bryony nodded. A potent mix of emotions swirled in her chest, regret and nostalgia mingling with fear and resentment. She shoved the words out past the knot in her throat. "They're the ones who pushed me away. They didn't accept my relationship with Maia. We'd no choice but to leave."

Ariel's face said that he understood. "I know. When I heard that Maia had left not just London, but Britain, I was… not happy." Bryony guessed that was an understatement. "It took me three months to track her movements back to the Morvann Islands. Then we had some trouble in London, which delayed me for a while." He paused and leaned back against the cushions. His shirt stretched over his torso in a distracting way. No doubt he had washboard abs under the light cotton fabric.

Damn it! She had to stop this! She dragged her eyes back to his face, and found it full of amusement as if he knew exactly what she'd been thinking.

And maybe he did. What with him being a warlock. She should have been horrified at the thought that he might be able to read her mind. Instead, a little flame of excitement sprang up in her belly.

She made an effort to concentrate on what he was saying. "You eventually went to the Islands, and discovered that Maia had run away with me?"

"Yes, Bryony." His voice had dropped into a purr. "And now I understand why." His eyes travelled all over her body, lingering on her legs and breasts. The flame in her loins grew hotter.

She swallowed. This was her cue to say that if he understood, all was well, and he could go back to the UK and leave them alone.

But she didn't want him to leave. Not yet. She cleared her throat. "They're very conservative on the islands. Even my Clan, the Benetynns. They never understood that I was attracted to women. When Maia came and we fell in love… things were hard."

Ariel's dark gaze was full of sympathy. "I get it. I'm not angry with Maia anymore. But she took something from me when she left London. Something of value. And I want it back."

A dull weight settled in Bryony's stomach, almost squashing the excitement. "Maia stole from you?" So that was what she'd been hiding. No wonder she'd been afraid of Ariel coming after her.

Ariel sighed. "I'd entrusted her with a powerful amulet and asked her to test its powers. She chose to take it to a remote part of Wales… the Morvann Islands." His lips curled in a half-smile. "Who could have predicted she'd fall in love with a gorgeous mermaid?"

He leaned towards Bryony and brushed a strand of hair from her face. The tiny contact was enough to reawaken the embers between her thighs. His eyes held hers, drawing her in, as if she were a planet suddenly caught in the orbit of a powerful sun. "The amulet gave her the opportunity to take you away, to a place where you could live and love in peace." He inclined his head towards her. "And now I know you, Bryony, I don't blame her." His breath caressed her face, as fresh as a breeze over a summer meadow. "I would have done the same."

All she could see was his mouth. All she could feel was how much she wanted it. As if in a dream, she brought her head nearer to his… and nearer… until her lips brushed his. Only a fleeting touch, but it reverberated in her entire body, filling her with trembling sparks of arousal.

His hand caught the back of her head, pulling her closer. His mouth captured hers, and his tongue parted her lips. A deep shiver shook her, and she surrendered to the kiss, opening her mouth wide so he could explore her better. He tasted delicious, like her first stolen sip of whisky when she was a teenager. Like the first bite into a forbidden fruit.

"What the hell do you two think you're doing?"

Maia's scream tore through the air, yanking Bryony out of her sensual daze. A tidal wave of shame slammed into her. She broke off the kiss and jumped to her feet to face her furious lover. "Maia—"

"Don't you 'Maia' me, you little tramp!" Her girlfriend planted her hands on her hips. Her face had turned beetroot red. "How could you do this to me? And with him!"

Bryony recoiled before her fury. There was nothing she could do or say. She'd been caught red-handed. Bitter guilt rose, choking her.

"It's my fault, Maia." Ariel spoke in a calm, reasonable tone from the sofa. "I wanted to seduce Bryony to get back at you. I put a spell on her. She wasn't herself."

He was lying. The only magic he'd used was his charm and good looks. Bryony opened her mouth to say as much, but Maia was already marching up to her former mentor, hands fisted, eyes blazing.

"You had no right to do that, Ariel."

He looked at her steadily, unruffled by her fury. "You're right. I should have waited until you got back… and asked for your permission."

Maia leaned until her nose was inches from his face. "I'll have you know that Bryony is special. She's not like the other girls."

Blood buzzed in Bryony's ears. Had she heard that right?

"Yes, Maia and I used to share girls." Ariel sounded amused. "So you see, you have nothing to feel embarrassed about, Bryony. I just jumped the gun a little."

Bryony's shame receded, replaced by growing excitement. Maia and Ariel, with another woman… with her… Pictures flashed through her mind. It was so wrong… naughty… and enticing.

Ariel lifted a hand. Maia flinched, but he only cupped her cheek. "I heard you in the taxi yesterday. You know I can listen to you talking at a distance. When I choose to." His thumb traced a circle on her skin. Maia's eyes grew heavy, half-lidded with… lust?

"You suggested that you and Bryony could pick up a man one night and bring him back home." Ariel's smile had a hint of the wolf in it. "But why wait for the night?"

Maia's lips parted. Her round breasts rose and fell under her thin blouse. Wet warmth bloomed between Bryony's thighs. Could she really have both Maia and Ariel? Here, now?

Maia gulped down air. "Is that why you came? Why you called me half an hour ago, and told me to come back home?"

Ariel's teeth flashed in his perfect, bronzed face. "It's one reason. The other one is, I'd like the amulet back. You know, the one you stole from me, that gives its wearer luck."

Luck! Bryony has often thought about Maia's big win at the casino the day they'd arrived in Las Vegas. She'd wondered if some divine being had intervened on their behalf. The reality was more prosaic. "You used the amulet to gamble?" she asked.

Maia bit her lip. "Yes. We needed money, baby. It was the only way I could see for us to build a new life together and give you what you need." She gestured at the room around them. "A nice house, a big pool… so you wouldn't suffer too much from leaving your home and family behind." Her anger seemed to have drained from her. She dug into the pocket of her jeans and pulled out a polished green stone, the size of a walnut.

Ariel extended his hand, and she dropped it into his palm. "I wanted to give it back to you, but I was afraid of facing you…" Her voice trailed off.

Ariel closed his fingers over the stone. When he opened his hand, the amulet had disappeared. "I was angry with you, but no longer. I understand that you did it for Bryony. For love."

A soft, warm feeling swept over Bryony. Maia had stolen for her. Maia had risked the wrath of a powerful warlock, for her. Thank the Goddess, it didn't look like Ariel wanted to punish her. Quite the contrary.

"I wish you'd told me, Maia," she said.

Her girlfriend hung her head. "I was ashamed. And I didn't want you to worry, baby. I never used the amulet again, after that win. I put it aside, in the hope that one day I could return it to its true owner." She lifted her gaze to Ariel's face. "Do you forgive me?"

He grinned. "Not only do I forgive you, I have a present for you and Bryony." He pulled an object from his pocket and showed it to them. It was a ring, made of a blue material that shone in the morning light like sapphire.

Maia gasped. "A love jewel! You'd give it to us? For real?"

Ariel's grin widened. "I have several. So yes, you can have it, as a token of my goodwill, and to show there are no hard feelings. But there's a condition."

Maia waited. Bryony's muscles tensed in anticipation, heightening the pleasurable tension at the apex of her thighs. A love jewel… for her and Maia. What did it do?

Ariel's gaze flicked to her as if he'd heard her unspoken question. "The jewel gives its wearer the ability to feel what their lover is feeling." His voice wrapped around her like silk. "You and Maia will experience each other's pleasure."

The sexual buzz grew and spread into her belly. She was like a fly, trapped in a spider's web, except she'd no desire to escape. She licked her lips. "And what do you want in return?"

His gaze speared her with heat. "You, Bryony."

Time slowed, then stopped. The world outside disappeared. It was as if she were stepping out of ordinary life into an enchanted forest, where this gorgeous man waited for her. But she couldn't go to him. Not without Maia's permission. She turned to her girlfriend, opened her mouth to ask the question, then found that her throat had gone dry. Embarrassment crept over her body, heating her skin… increasing her need.

Maia's tongue peeked at the corner of her mouth. "It's OK. You can have him, baby. Who could resist him?" Her wicked grin lit up the room. "And I'll join in."

Dizziness swept over Bryony. She wasn't sure she'd heard right. As if in a dream, she glanced at Ariel.

He crooked a finger. "You've heard your girlfriend. Come here."

Her feet moved of their own accord and carried her towards him. He reached out and pulled her onto his lap. "Straddle me."

The command sent a thrill through her. She obeyed, gripping his shoulders, and shivered when her bare skin touched his long legs. Now her damp mound was only inches away from the straining bulge in his jeans. Lust gripped her tighter until every nerve in her body thrummed with expectation.

He took her hand and slid the blue ring on her fourth finger. He sang under his breath, in a language Bryony didn't understand. But she recognised magic when she heard it. "What spell is this?" she asked. A hint of anxiety sharpened the edge of her excitement. Magic was always a little dangerous. Just like the man who was about to possess her.

Ariel finished his incantation and gave her his magnetic smile. "You'll see... when Maia gets closer."

Bryony turned her head towards her girlfriend, but Ariel cupped her neck and pulled her back towards him. "No. I want you to focus on me until she joins us. Understood?"

"Yes." She almost added "Master," but stopped herself just in time. He was using magic now, she was sure of it. Unspoken spells in his voice, that compelled her to do exactly what he wanted. Her blood pounded in her veins, spreading a web of yearning through her flesh. She was at his mercy. And she loved it. She gazed at him, losing herself in the dark fire of his eyes... relishing the power he had over her.

His hands slid under her skirt and caressed her thighs. Scarlet flames of desire leaped and burned her skin. Her sex throbbed with a need so acute she gasped. His long fingers moved higher and glanced against her damp curls, sending a shock of electricity through her. Ariel chuckled. The silvery sound was like a running brook, washing reality away. She was fully immersed in the dream now, living out her fantasy.

"Maia, this naughty girl isn't wearing any knickers." Ariel's voice had grown husky. "Do you let her get away with that?"

Suddenly Maia was right behind her. Bryony felt her knees press against the small of her back. Maia's arms encircled her and she captured her breasts, massaging them through the flimsy fabric. Bryony's already hard tips tightened even further. "No bra either," Maia purred. "So naughty. We have to punish her." She dipped a hand under the low neckline of the dress and pinched a nipple. Fire streamed from Bryony's breast down to her belly. She squirmed under the sweet torture, but her lovers would have no mercy. Maia rolled the sensitive tip between her fingers, just as Ariel cupped Bryony's mound and pressed down on her swollen clit. Pleasure scorched her, and she cried aloud. "Yes, oh, yes!"

"Take her, Ariel. I want you to enter her. I want to feel you inside her… inside me." Maia's voice, breathy and urgent in her ear.

Ariel withdrew his hand, and Bryony heard the click of his belt… a rustling of fabric. She looked down, and gasped at the sight of his magnificent cock, ready for her. She lifted herself on her knees, trembling, a tiny stab of fear piercing the storm of her desire. She'd never done it with a man before. This was a real member, not one made of magic and air. Would it hurt?

Ariel's hands seized her hips, positioning her just right. "I've got you. Don't worry, I'll take care of you." His soft voice erased the fear, leaving only her devouring hunger. She lowered herself onto him. The head of his cock pushed against her opening, and her body welcomed him with slippery, wet warmth. Inch by inch he penetrated her, deeper and deeper, burrowing into her molten core.

He paused. "Tell me if I'm hurting you." In answer she moaned and slid down on his shaft, taking him in until he filled her completely.

Maia's hands tightened on her breasts. "Oh baby, I can feel him… Oh, that's so good." Bryony's pussy clenched around the cock that was lodged so deep in her, and tongues of delight licked every cell in her body. The knowledge that Maia was sharing the experience intensified her pleasure, driving her towards the edge. She rose on her knees and slammed down, whimpering as her mound splayed against Ariel's taut male flesh. He groaned and pumped into her, each stroke rocking her body with a wild, animal passion.

Then a new sensation surged into her sex. Somehow, she knew that Maia was touching herself. She could feel her fingers against her clit, stroking and rubbing, sending sweet pangs of bliss into every part of her. She was one with Maia and one with Maia's pleasure. The twin waves of ecstasy crashed over her… rolled and tumbled her… filled her to the brim… until she exploded at last, screaming her joy in a soul-shattering release.

***

Bryony opened her eyes. The golden light of late afternoon seeped through the curtains. She must have dozed for a few hours. At her side, Maia sighed in her sleep. Her long eyelashes fluttered, then she rolled over and burrowed deeper under the covers. Her breath grew even again.

A glow suffused Bryony's entire body, warmer and brighter than the declining sun outside. She, Maia and Ariel had made love until lunch, in every combination and position imaginable. They'd paused for a bite to eat, then they'd tumbled into the king-size bed for more fun and games. At last, they'd fallen asleep, tangled in each other's arms. The pleasure had been more intense than ever, thanks to Ariel's gift. Bryony turned the blue ring around her finger, admiring its sparkle.

But the bond between her and Maia went much deeper than the flesh, and somehow during those golden hours, it had grown stronger. She could feel it into her very soul. Bryony stretched, relishing the tingling weariness in her limbs. Perhaps it was magic. Perhaps it was because Maia had given her what she wanted and held nothing back. She knew now that Maia would never leave her. Not for Ariel, not for anyone.

The other side of the bed was empty. Where was the warlock? Bryony pushed the covers off and got up. She grabbed her silk dressing-gown on the back of the door and padded out. The house was cool and quiet, but a faint hum emanated from the kitchen and the aroma of coffee. She went downstairs.

Ariel, seated at the table, greeted her with a smile. "Fancy a cup?" He gestured at the state-of-the-art coffee machine on the gleaming marble counter.

Bryony shook her head. "I won't sleep tonight if I take caffeine now. But I could murder a muffin."

He pushed the tin of cakes towards her. He'd obviously showered and shaved and looked delicious enough to eat. His white shirt, open at the neck, revealed a small love bite, red against the smooth bronzed skin. She couldn't remember whether she or Maia had put it there.

She nibbled at her muffin and watched him drink his coffee. For a few moments, she indulged in a fantasy. The three of them living here in Las Vegas, doing magical things by day and sexy things by night… But she knew it was only a dream.

"How long are you staying in Vegas?"

He put his cup down. "Sadly, I have to fly back tomorrow morning. I have business in town tonight with some local warlocks. I'll stay with one of them." He checked his phone. "I called a taxi. It should be here in a few minutes."

"Oh." The pang of disappointment was sharp. She'd hoped he might stay a few days… or the night at least. She abandoned her muffin, her appetite gone.

His smile lit up his face and put some warmth back into her heart. "Sorry. I'd have loved to spend more time with you and Maia. But perhaps you could come to London? You'll both be very welcome."

"I'd love that." Bryony's mood lifted. She pictured herself on a plane with Maia, flying over the Atlantic. Walking hand in hand through Hyde Park, taking selfies before the Houses of Parliament. "I could perhaps visit my family on the way. If you think they're not so pissed with me anymore."

"They would love that." Ariel handed her a business card. "You have my address and number on there. Give me a call when you and Maia are in town."

Bryony turned the small square of thick, embossed card in her fingers. It seemed to shimmer in the declining light as if some fairy dust had settled on it. "I will."

Ariel took her hand and kissed it. "Thank you, Bryony."

"Thank you," she whispered. "Before you came, I worried that perhaps Maia would get bored with me. Now I know she won't."

Ariel stood. "She loves you, Bryony. She doesn't need a magical ring to do that. You can be sure of it."

His phone buzzed. "My taxi is waiting outside."

She walked with him through the door and down the garden path. Shadows lay long over the grass. The jasmine shrubs filled the evening air with their heady scent. Ariel stopped at the gate. It opened for him without a sound. "What you two have is very precious." Was that a touch of wistfulness in his voice? "Enjoy it, and each other."

"I will. For as long as we both shall live." Bryony gazed at his back as he strode to the waiting taxi. Just before he opened the door, he turned and waved. *Goodbye, Bryony. Or rather, au revoir.* He didn't say the words, but she heard them in her head.

She stood in the fragrant garden and watched until the car disappeared into the setting sun. Then she closed the gate and went back into the house. She was going to wake Maia up. Then, over dinner, she would propose to her.

Because Ariel was right. What they had was precious, and she didn't want to hide their love anymore. She wanted to shout it from the rooftops. If she was going to take Maia back to the UK, to see her family, it wouldn't be as her girlfriend. It would be as her wife.

Because love comes in many shapes, and not all of them have a tail… or a penis. It was time for the merfolk of the Morvann Islands to understand that.

The End

James
Callie Carmen

Chapter One

James

One brief conversation had sent my world into a tailspin. For the past two years, I'd been in an online relationship with Dale. The highs and lows had been a roller coaster ride of emotions. One minute I'd been lost in his beautiful words of love, and the next I'd been furious over another of his cancellations.

We'd met virtually when he'd seen me on Tinder and contacted me. We had wanted to meet right away, but our schedules hadn't matched. I'd decided to see if he had a Facebook, Instagram, or other social media profile. I'd found him on Facebook, which had the same pictures as I'd seen on Tinder, only more of them. It seemed natural, a few months into the relationship, to date Dale online.

From then on, when I met a hot guy, I'd hook him up with my best friend, Samuel. Sam meant the world to me, and I wanted him to be happy even if it wouldn't be with me. I confided in him about Dale and just about everything in my life, and he did the same with me. The only thing I hid from Samuel was how much I loved him.

I knew that would never happen. I was just a receptionist at an accounting firm, flamboyant and outgoing. He was a lawyer at the second largest law firm in Detroit, reserved and introspective. He dated successful, gorgeous men, but never more than a few times. He was focused on making partner in his firm. He wasn't about to look my way, because I wasn't his type.

Sure, I'd been called handsome, almost pretty, but I was far from successful. I was all about a long-term relationship. I had only dated a few people and always long-term until they hadn't worked out. Mainly because my heart belonged to Sam. I would never hit on him though because it would ruin our relationship. We wanted different things.

As far as friends go, we were the best. I'd force him to tell me about his week, which I knew helped him relieve the stress of his high-powered job. Then I'd prattle on about mine, and he'd always end up laughing from my stories about the women I worked with and their crazy issues with men. He helped to calm me down and I helped liven him up.

Sam and I were about to watch our favorite show, *Schitt's Creek*. We had gotten a late start watching the series, which had already ended, but better late than never. We were both crazy about the sour attitude, dramatic flair, and outrageous facial expressions of the character David Rose. He cracked us up. The aroma of buttered popcorn wafted from the kitchen to the living room as I handed a bowl of popcorn and a soda to Samuel.

He hadn't approved of my long-distance online dating. He thought I was wasting my time on Dale. So it didn't surprise me when he asked, "Was the six-hour drive to meet Dale yesterday worth the trip?"

I hadn't wanted to ruin the excitement of what predicament David would get into this week. I'd planned to tell him what happened with Dale after the show.

I plopped my fists on my hips. "Fine. I'll tell you. But you're ruining my buzz."

Sam's lips were closed and pulled to one side.

I sat on the couch with him and huffed. "Four hours into my drive, he had the nerve to text me that his car had broken down. He had his car towed, and a friend had to give him a ride home. I was mad as a hatter." I closed my fist and punch the arm of the couch.

"Good thing it was a Sunday. If I had missed work, I would have dropped him right then."

Samuel put his bare feet up on my coffee table and took a sip of his drink. "I don't know what you see in that guy. I think he's married or hiding something from you. The guy won't even Facetime or Zoom with you. Get rid of him."

"Great minds think alike. Bella at work agrees with you. Today she told me about a show called *Catfish*. Before you got here, I watched a couple of episodes. Nev, the man that runs the show is—"

I fanned myself.

Sam grimaced.

"Nev showed how to do a reverse image search on Google. It's supposed to show everywhere that image has appeared on the internet so I can see if the info matches up. If not, I can look at his media sites to see who he's chatting with and contact them to see what they know about Dale. You can even research a person's phone number."

Samuel put his feet on the floor and leaned forward. "What are you waiting for? Let's load up some of his pictures and find out who this bastard is."

"Wow. Tell me how you really feel." My stomach flip-flopped.

I pulled up the reverse search and uploaded a headshot of Dale. My stomach churned as several pictures and videos of a German male model and fitness trainer appeared on the screen. There were videos of him walking the runway in Europe, magazine photo spreads in GQ, and fitness videos of him speaking German.

"Dale" had taken the casual pictures of this guy walking his dog, sitting on a park bench, and at the beach and used them for his Tinder and Facebook photos. There was no way the man that I spoke with on the phone had a German accent.

He'd been lying to me for TWO FREAKING YEARS. Pain shot through my forehead.

Samuel wrapped his arms around me and pulled me in for a hug. I felt his heart racing. "I'm sorry, babe."

I should have cried, but Samuel's words and warm embrace filled me with pleasure, and the pain subsided. Besides, I'd had doubts about Dale long before this. What hurt most was the wasted two years, and it embarrassed me that I'd been so stupid.

"James, I want you to call that bastard right now. Tell him it's over if he doesn't meet with you."

"Now? Why?"

"Yes. Now. I have a few choice words for him, and I want to do it face-to-face. Depending on what he has to say for himself, I may contact this Hans model. He might just want me or another lawyer to represent him in a claim against Dale for misappropriation of likeness."

I swallowed hard to choke down the love I felt for Samuel.

"If he agrees to meet, I'll be right there by your side."

I picked up my phone and hit Dale's number. He picked up on the second ring and I put him on speaker.

"Baby. I was just thinking about you. I'm sorry yesterday didn't work out. I miss you."

Another lie. God, how had I fallen for his bullshit? I cringed.

"Good, I'm glad you miss me, because if you don't meet with me, we're over."

I heard his deep intake of breath. "Baby, you don't mean it?"

"I do."

"But—"

"No but."

"Okay, we'll meet, but you will not like what you see. Please don't hate me. I really love you. I can be at the diner near your office in twenty minutes."

I jumped off my seat. "What the hell?" I had driven four hours there and four hours back home yesterday. I wanted to kill him!

Sam put his hand up to my lips and shook his head.

"Fine. You'd better be there."

"Okay," he whispered.

Sam and I looked at each other with our mouths hung open.

A few minutes later, the two of us entered the diner. I looked around and saw a few couples, and an old guy at the counter talking to the waitress. Could that be the guy? He looked old enough to be my grandfather. I shook my head. No way. Far in the back, I saw my mortal enemy from high school, Mark Dane. He had the nerve to stand and wave us back to his table. The man had bullied me through four years of high school. At one point, it had gotten so bad I had wanted to kill myself. Even now I shook with hate for the evil spawn of the devil.

Sam bumped my shoulder with his. "Let's go." He walked past me right towards Mark.

"Sam," I screeched. But he wasn't having it. He swung his arm in the air, urging me to follow him toward the man he thought was Dale.

My legs dragged with each step I took towards Mark, the last person I wanted to see right now. Sam put out his hand. "I'm Samuel. You must be Dale. You have a lot of explaining to do and it had better be good, or I might have to mess up that pretty face of yours."

Mark ignored Sam. His eyes were on me, I noticed, as I got closer, that they were welled up with tears. Samuel sat down in the booth as I reached the table. The evil spawn reached out to hug me.

I took one step back. "Don't touch me." My voice was seething.

"Please. I'd like to explain why I did what I did to you."

God help me. I had always wondered how anyone could be as mean-spirited as Mark had been. My curiosity wouldn't let this opportunity get past me. I sat down. "Fine, but you'd better be quick about it. We're meeting someone. He should be here any minute."

Samuel looked at me like I had two heads. He had no idea who Mark was and was probably thinking we were with Dale. Or was Mark actually Dale? No one could be that big of an asshole. He'd have to be mental to carry on his torture into adulthood.

"We're waiting." I tapped my foot on the tile floor.

The server came over with a pot of coffee. Would you gentlemen like a cup of Joe?

"No." My tone was harsh. I looked up at her. "Sorry."

"Yes, please." Sam smiled. The woman practically drooled over his sparkling eyes, full lips and perfect teeth. I couldn't blame her. I had fantasies about him often. She flipped over the cup and poured the coffee, then scurried off.

Mark drummed his fingers on the table. I wanted to reach over and slap his hand to make him stop. "Back in high school, I lived with my father. He was an authoritarian. I followed his rules, or I was beaten." He shrugged and looked at the table. "He was also a homophobe. He called people like you sissy, girlie man, pansy, fairy, fudge packer, faggot—"

"We get the idea your father's an asshole. Kind of like you. Get to the point." I glared at him and crossed my arms.

The pained grimace on his face almost cracked the thick shield I had over my heart.

Sam put his hand on my thigh and squeezed it.

Fine, I'll be nicer. "Go on."

"I saw what happened to you our freshmen year when you trusted your friends to keep your secret so your parents wouldn't find out." He stopped drumming his fingers and looked at Sam then back to me. "We all know how that went. Still, I was so proud of you. I admired you, but I became jealous of you. I hated that you could be yourself and no longer hide, but I couldn't."

I didn't have a neighborhood friend that went to a private high school. One that had wonderful parents, that would take me in when my father kicked me out, like you did. You had Samuel. I had no one to turn to. I couldn't tell anyone that I was gay. If they had let it slip and my father found out, he would have killed me. There was no way that man was going to have a faggot for a son. I felt flawed, unworthy to be loved, ashamed, and was living in fear. Those feelings turned into scorn for you. I wanted what you had. Only I had to worry about my security and couldn't have it."

My stomach groaned out loud.

"I mocked, ridiculed, and belittled you. To make myself feel better."

I sneered at him. The memories of his abuse were seared into my brain.

"It didn't work. I didn't feel better. I felt worse. By the time I figured that out, I had already been accepted into the one group at school that was exactly like my bigoted father, and I became depressed. Those assholes I hung out with offered me drugs. I took them to help ease the pain. They botched my one attempt at an overdose suicide when they rushed me to the hospital.

"For months, I had to listen to my father tell me how hard he had to work to keep a roof over our head and food on the table. How he couldn't believe that I'd repay him by trying to kill myself. How humiliated he was that his friends knew his son had tried to kill himself. And my favorite: 'Next time finish the job or don't do it at all.' I wouldn't give him the satisfaction, so I never tried it again."

I unfolded my arms. If he truly regretted what he'd done to me, and if he took responsibility for it, not blaming his father or anyone else, and was sorry for the pain he'd caused me, I thought I could forgive him. I'd never forget, but I could forgive him, and that would give me a healthier and more hopeful future for myself. I sighed.

"It took to the middle of our senior year for me to understand that my feelings of respect and admiration for you were love. But it was too late. By then you hated me for all the pain I'd caused you." His posture sagged.

This guy was screwed up in the head. Was he a stalker, a loon, or maybe both? A crazy who knew where I worked. Where I lived. First, he was proud of me. Then he admired me. He was jealous of me. Back to admiring. All the while torturing me. And now he loved me. A strong inner feeling of foreboding rubbed my nerves raw.

"I call bullshit," I voiced loudly. "That isn't love, that's—"

I looked away, sick at the sight of him.

"You got one thing right. I hated you."

Sam rubbed my shoulder and calmed me a bit.

Mark covered his face with both hands and slowly slid them back down. The color had drained from his face. "When I finished college, I wrote my father a letter letting him know I was gay. He called me and left a message that I was no longer his son. If I ever darkened his door, he'd kill me.

"For years I've regretted all the terrible things I did to you. I hoped that someday you could forgive me. When I saw your name and picture on Tinder, it felt like fate. I had to contact you. To build a relationship with you. I wanted you to know the person I'd become. We got along so well that I hoped you'd fall in love with me and love me as much as I loved you. I hoped you could forgive me. So many times I wanted to stop hiding and let you know I was Dale, but I was afraid I'd lose you."

I was frozen in my seat. I couldn't even speak. *Liar. Poser. So many intimate conversations.* A burning sensation spread up my esophagus to my throat and left a sour taste in my mouth. Four years of torture. No, six. Mind games. All the times he said I love you had left me hopeful I could fall in love when we finally met in person. I must have looked like an idiot to Samuel. I was beyond naïve. I was—

Sam leaned over the table, bared his teeth, and grabbed Mark by the collar. "Are you trying to tell the kindest, most considerate man I know that not only are you the guy that tortured him in high school, but that you're also Dale, the bastard that has been stringing him along for the past two years? You robbed him of any chance of falling in love with an actual person, not some figment of his imagination, for two freaking years. You're not worthy to shine his shoes." Sam's whispered words were far more frightening than any screamed in anger.

The ice that was forming around my heart because of Mark or Dale, whatever he was calling himself these days, melted. Sam's words were beautiful. I hadn't known he felt those things about me. He really was the most wonderful friend a person could ever have.

He barely ever spoke unless it was about work. Or to tell me that another one of the blind dates I had sent him on had been a disaster. "Don't you dare set me up again," he always said. Of course, I never listened. I wanted him to be happy. I wasn't the love-him-and-leave type like Sam had always dated. I'd only had three past relationships, each lasting close to two years. During those years Sam was doing the opposite. He rarely dated, and when he did, it was over in a couple of days, or less. Dare I say—wham, bam, thank you, man.

I wanted forever with Sam, but if he wanted me at all, it would be for his usual casual sex. We'd be left with a giant elephant in the room after the intimacy was over. Besides, I wasn't the successful business suit type of guy that he normally dated. Our friendship wouldn't survive dating. I would never be able to handle him moving on to the next man. That would rip my heart out. So I kept how I felt a secret.

I placed my hand over Sam's arm. "We found our catfish. It's getting late and we still have a movie to watch. Let's go." I stood, he released Mark's shirt, and without another word to the man, we left.

When we got to my apartment, I deleted my Tinder and Facebook accounts. In the morning, I'd be changing my cell phone number. I never wanted to hear from that catfish again.

Before we sat on the couch to watch the movie, Samuel pulled me into his arms and held me tight to his body. I knew he was trying to make sure I was okay. What he didn't know was that being pressed to his hard body was making me grow hard. I was afraid he'd feel my attraction, which would embarrass him. So I pulled back.

"The worst part is that if Mark had told me after high school what he had been going through for those four years, I would have forgiven him and spent time with him. Maybe we could have started a real relationship. But there's no way that can happen now. I'd never be able to trust him. The tragedy is that we both end the past two years with scarred hearts." I sniffed. "Thank God I hadn't fallen in love with him."

My friend of few words sighed.

Chapter Two

James

"Aren't you a ray of sunshine, out here singing like a bird." Tessa smiled.

I was in a fabulous mood for someone that had just broken off a two-year relationship. It felt like the weight of the world had been lifted off my shoulders.

"Bright-eyed and bushy-tailed." I dropped the pen I'd been using into the pen dispenser.

"Perfect. I'm glad you're in a good mood." Tessa, my boss and friend, dragged me back to her office to help her out with something. I was ready, willing, and able.

"James, I pray you can help me. You know that gorgeous friend of yours? The one with the blond hair and blue eyes?"

I stood in her doorway and raised a brow. "You must mean Samuel. Why do you ask?"

She rolled the straw wrapper that was on her desk with her fingers. "I need a date for Violet and Joseph's wedding this weekend."

"Girl, you know he's one of my gay friends, right? I thought you'd been drooling over that hunk of a man, Anthony."

"Yes, and that's why I need Samuel's help."

I put my fists on my hips and looked at her like she was crazy. "Girlfriend, you're not making any sense. I thought Anthony was going to the wedding."

"He is, but… the man moves at a snail's pace." She crushed the straw paper into a ball and tossed it toward the trash. "He's interested in me. My friends told me they could tell by the way he acted and the things he said when he was around me. But he hasn't asked me out. Joseph and Violet's wedding would have been the perfect opportunity, but he didn't ask." She combed her fingers through her hair.

She took a deep breath, then huffed. "Jaq told us that her brother hasn't dated since his divorce over a year ago. That he's been working hard to make his restaurant successful."

I swooshed my hand toward her. "He's done that. So why wouldn't he go after you?"

She shrugged her shoulders. "Anthony told Joseph that he's taking his time this go around, so he doesn't make the same mistake he made with his first marriage."

"Are you telling me that hot man hasn't had sex for over a year? His balls are going to shrivel up and die. Are you sure he's straight?" I teased.

"I didn't say he hadn't had sex. I'm saying he hasn't dated anyone."

I smirked. "And how does Jaq feel about you manipulating her brother? I thought she'd put up a roadblock when she found out because of your boy-crazed days in college."

"Good question. I didn't get a chance to tell you what happened at dinner last night. My friends forced me to tell her how I felt about her brother. The look on Jaq's face made me queasy. I told her I was head over heels crazy about Anthony and that was the reason I hadn't been dating."

"Drama. You go, girl. I want all the dirt." I plopped down on the seat in front of her desk.

She smiled because she knew how much I love to gossip.

"At first, she accused me of secretly dating her brother and wanted to know why I would do such a thing."

I slapped the top of her desk. "Oh, this is getting good. What did you say? Did you get angry?"

"I told her I would never do such a thing. Then she stuck out her chin and demanded to know what I was going to do about it."

I grimaced. "What do you mean?"

She laughed. "That's what I asked. She told me he wasn't a pursuer of women and never had been. He was a driven man who put most of his energy into his dreams of having a successful restaurant, and he was a painfully slow mover when it came to asking a woman out. Then she asked me again what I was going to do about it. At that point, my heart raced."

She leaned forward and steepled her hands.

"She told me I was a good friend. And, sure, at the beginning of our senior year she'd been worried about my trolling for men. At the time, I had been dealing with my worst daddy-daughter issues."

"Oh, please. Who hasn't done some sleeping around in their younger years?"

She puffed out her lips. "Well, Jaq hadn't, but don't you dare call her a prude the next time you see her because she isn't one."

I placed my hand over my wounded heart. "Who, me? I'd never do such a thing."

She melted back onto her seat. "Well, it wasn't my finest period in life. Then she said I was the nicest, smartest, most beautiful woman inside and out that she'd ever known." Her eyes welled up.

I nodded. "Damn straight you are."

"Thank you, James. She wants me to date her thick-headed brother."

"Of course she does. Your outgoing, fiery personality is what that man needs. So how would having Samuel as your date help you get Anthony?"

She leaned forward and took hold of my hand. "You're not going to believe this, but according to Jaq, we need to make him jealous enough to get him to ask me out."

I gave her a devious smile. "Hmm. So Samuel would be the bait that gets Anthony to wake up and get moving in on all the fineness that is you. I think you're all nuts, but I happen to know that Samuel is free this Saturday, because he was going to hang with me until I had to leave for the wedding. I'll hook the two of you up."

"You're the best."

"I hope this doesn't backfire on you. You could lose Anthony if he doesn't like being manipulated."

"We'll have to make sure he doesn't find out. I've already waited seven months for him to notice me and make his move. We ladies think that's long enough. Don't you?"

"Take it from a man that just wasted two years of his life. I agree, and that is why you should have taken all that fineness of yours and moved on to greener pastures. Stop waiting around for this guy. No matter how hot he is, no one's worth waiting that long for."

"I would normally agree with you, but there's so much more to Anthony than his good looks. I'm going to give it this one last try. If it doesn't work, I'll take your advice and move on. I'll be heartbroken, but I owe it to myself to find what Jaq, Carlie, and Violet have. True love is out there for me, and for you too. I feel it."

I looked up at the ceiling. "From your lips to God's ears."

Samuel

It shocked me when James asked me to be Tessa's date for Violet and Joseph's wedding. I was used to him fixing me up with one guy after the next. But now he was fixing me up with a woman.

The man was willing to be exclusive with someone he'd never met, a total stranger, for two freaking years, but he'd never looked my way for a relationship. Every time he fixed me up with another guy, I felt sick to my stomach because it was him I wanted. It was so frustrating. Each time I was ready to tell him how I felt, he'd announce he'd met someone. I'd spend the next couple of years waiting for their relationship to go south, only to have a new one start up again within days. I'd gulp back sorrow and tell him I was happy for him. God, it was like he couldn't be without someone for more than a minute. I always wanted a bit of time after one of his break-ups because I didn't want to be the rebound guy. Those relationships always ended in tears. I couldn't bring that to his attention because it might build a wedge between us that was too big to repair. I needed him in my life, even if it was only as a friend, but I wanted so much more. Maybe this time he'd take a long enough breather for me to make my move.

The sun was setting by the time Violet and Joseph's wedding ceremony was ending. I felt a tug at my heart when I saw her sister walking her down the aisle, Tessa had told me that Violet had lost her parents and grandparents at a young age. There wasn't a dry eye in the place when Joseph expressed his never-ending love during his vows to her. When he bent down and kissed Violet's stomach, where their baby grew, I held my breath. I wanted to adopt children one day, but I wanted to be married first and I wanted it to be to James. I hoped it might be possible now that Dale was out of the way. Tingles ran up my spine.

I looked across the aisle and caught Anthony looking our way. If looks could kill, I'd be dead. I'd been playing my part as Tessa's date perfectly. I'd held her hand as we walked to our seats. Whenever I spoke to her, I bent down and whispered in her ear. To top it off, I kissed the back of her hand during the vows, which was what Anthony had seen. The poor guy practically had steam coming out of his ears. The look on his face was so irate that it reminded me of how I felt when James sent me off with another blind date and spent his evening talking on the phone with Dale. It hurt like a stab to the gut. It made me feel guilty that I was causing Anthony that kind of pain.

Tessa had pointed out Patrick, Jaq's husband. He was sitting next to Anthony. Patrick leaned in, pointed at me and whispered something to his brother-in-law. Anthony gave him a dirty look, then turned back towards me. His icy stare was making it chilly in here. I hoped Tessa knew what she was doing with this farce.

I turned back in time to see Joseph and Violet's first kiss as man and wife. We all cheered.

James was sitting on my other side and squeezed my bicep. "Someday I want that too," he whispered. I wasn't one for showing emotions, but I had to choke back tears. I prayed I'd be the one to give him marriage and that kind of undying love.

***

The reception was tense for me and not much fun. I was seated at a table with James on one side of Tessa and me on the other. Olivia, one of the best friends of James's bosses, was seated on the other side of James. She was stunning. She had a short pixie hairstyle with bangs that fell over her eyes now and then. My stomach tightened every time James brushed them back from her sweet face. They were laughing, having lots of fun. He was always attracted to those in need, and from what I heard, that was Olivia. It was one of the things I loved about him. He was so caring, but right now I was jealous as hell that it wasn't me he was doing those things with instead of her.

It was my understanding that several months ago her ex-boyfriend had raped her and taken her virginity. I bet being here with a gay man helped make her feel comfortable. James didn't have a date either, so I was kind of happy they had each other. Kind of.

Anthony was seated directly across from me, next to one of Violet's single co-workers. He wasn't saying two words to the woman, even though she was practically throwing herself at him.

I could see his interest in Tessa by the way he stared at me like I was the devil himself. James was going to owe me one for this charade. If Anthony wasn't full of steam, he would have noticed that my attention was on James, not Tessa. I'd better cool it, or I'd mess things up for Tessa.

I bent down and whispered in Tessa's ear. "Thank God the man doesn't have laser eyes, or I'd be dead." We both laughed, and I grabbed her hand. I rubbed the back with my thumb. It was pretty noisy with the music playing, but I could have sworn I heard Anthony growl. The woman next to him sat back in her seat away from him. Tessa, on the other hand, seemed drawn to him and leaned forward. She quivered, and I covered her hand to help steady her, hopefully before Anthony saw how he affected her.

James pulled Olivia from her seat and dragged her to the dance floor for a slow song. I figured I'd kill two birds with one stone. I could keep an eye on James and make Anthony jealous at the same time.

I stood. "May I have this dance?" I held my hand out for Tessa.

"I'd love to." Out of the corner of my eye, I saw Anthony head over to Patrick. He took a seat next to him. He had no idea that Patrick was in on our pretend date. If he had gone over to complain about me, I knew he wouldn't be getting any sympathy from his brother-in-law. It made me chuckle.

As the next slow song began, I spotted Patrick pushing Anthony towards the dance floor. I could make out, "Now or never." He looked back and gave Patrick a disgusted expression, then headed toward me.

I leaned down and whispered. "It's working."

She smiled.

I felt a tap on my shoulder. We stopped dancing and turned to Anthony.

"Hope you don't mind, but I'd like to cut in."

I glowered at him. "Yeah, I mind. Who are you?"

Tessa took a deep breath and waited for Anthony's reply.

"I'm the guy who's been sitting across from you for the last hour, and it's none of your—"

She patted my shoulder. "It's okay. He's my best friend Jaq's brother, and he's completely harmless."

"Then you're okay to dance with him?"

"Yes. Thank you."

I handed her off to Anthony, who wrapped his arms around her waist and pulled her into his body instead of taking her hand and placing it in his. She let out a squeak.

My attention turned to James. He had Olivia close enough to him that her breasts were pressed up against his chest. What the hell? The song playing was our song, "All of Me" by John Legend. James didn't know it was our song, but to me it told our story so far, and where I wished it would end. The song starts out mentioning the lover's smart mouth, which screamed James to me and always made me smile. And no matter what brought him down, I'd be there for him like he was for me. It talks about risking all his love on this one person, and he knew it would be hard but worth it. It was a beautiful love song playing for them when it should be me in his arms. My stomach ached and my shoulders slumped.

As I walked off the dance floor, I overheard Anthony speaking to Tess. "Harmless. Hah. What are you doing with him?"

I knew just how he felt. Why was James being so chummy with Olivia? I knew I was being ridiculous, but I couldn't help it. I was sick of waiting. Now that Dale was out of his life, I wasn't going to give him more than a week to get back on his feet. There was no way I was taking the chance that he'd meet someone else again. Rebound guy or not, I was going to take my chances and let the chips fall where they may.

When the song ended, Anthony pulled away from Tessa and she grabbed his tie. He turned towards the door and, little by little, his tie slid out of her grasp. He walked away, leaving her standing in the middle of the dance floor surrounded by happy couples, including Olivia and James. This night sucked.

It looked like their plan to make Anthony jealous had failed miserably. James had told me that if this ruse didn't work, Tessa was going to move on because she felt she'd given Anthony enough of her life with nothing in return.

When I poured my guts out to James the following week, if it didn't go as I hoped it would, then maybe it would be time for me to do the same. James may never see me as anything more than a friend. All I wanted to do was get the hell out of here. Thank God, Tessa wanted to do the same thing.

When I got home, I was exhausted. My pipe dream of a life with James might have been over. I'd have to live with the broken heart. Maybe someday someone equally special would come into my life.

Chapter Three

James

The week after the wedding had dragged. Sam had been busy with work all week, which was unusual. At least I'd see him tonight. Unfortunately, this weekend he'd be with another blind date that I had set him up on. I wanted him to find the one, but I was always relieved that the guy wasn't right for him. I knew it was wrong of me to feel elated about that, but I was.

Anthony had called and said he was coming over later in the day to meet with Tessa to go over his restaurant accounts. I was beaming when I told Tessa the good news. I was floored with her reply.

"Can't Carlie meet with him?"

"No can do. She already has an appointment booked with another client. Besides, I thought you were nuts about this guy."

She snarled at me.

I put my hands on my hips. "Isn't that why you took Samuel to the wedding? To make Anthony jealous?"

"Okay, I'll see him."

I smiled ear to ear.

"While we're on the subject of Samuel, did you know he has a major crush on you?"

I blew raspberries. "I wish. He's my best friend." I felt myself blush. "Did you even look at that man? He's gorgeous. Besides, he goes for powerful, sophisticated men. He'd never be interested in me in that way."

"Yes, he is. I watched him at the wedding. Whenever you talked, he hung on every word. Even though you're gay, when you slow danced with Olivia, and you two laughed and chatted, a big old green-eyed monster came out of him. At one point, I thought he was going to walk out on me, because you had your hand on Olivia's hand, and you bent over and whispered in her ear. He looked hurt, and I heard him groan."

I blew out air and gave a hand gesture of dismissal.

"Fine. You don't have to believe me, but I think it's time that you talk with him before you lose a good friend. If you're still looking for Mr. Right, I think you already have him."

She poked me in the chest. "You need to open your eyes."

"My God, girl, I've had a crush on him for years. If you're right, I must have hurt him so many times."

"What are you talking about?"

I put my hand over my mouth and talked between my spread fingers. "I've been fixing him up with hot, successful guys for the past year, and they never work out. I fixed him up with someone for tomorrow night." I cringed, thinking about how rejected Samuel must have felt.

"Oh, James."

"You better be right, because he's coming over tonight to hang out. I'm letting you know now that I'm leaving early today. I'm going to make him dinner and buy him his favorite wine. After dinner, I'm going to corner him in my kitchen, kiss the hell out of him, and then suck him dry."

She put her hand up. "I don't need the details, thank you very much."

"Like you never sucked a man dry. Pleassse." I bit my thumbnail. "If you're wrong, I'll most likely lose my best friend."

"I know I'm right, but are you sure you shouldn't talk with him before you jump his bones?"

"No way. He's not the touchy-feely kind of man and hates to talk about his feelings. Action would be appreciated, so that's what I'll do."

"Okay, I hope you have better luck than me." She squeezed my arm. "Good luck, hon."

I gave her a closed-lipped smile.

***

The remaining four hours should have flown by, but they didn't. My stomach was churning with nerves and excitement. The possibility to be with a man like Samuel filled me with joy.

When my parents threw me out for being gay, he had come through for me. He'd convinced his mother to take me in. During the bullying and the last two years with Dale, he had been supportive. He was a trusted friend who always had my back. When he'd told Mark that I was the kindest and most considerate man he knew it had overwhelmed me with gratitude and love. It had made my heart sing.

But it wasn't those things that were the most important. When we were together, we were both fully engaged in our conversation, and we understood each other. We didn't always agree, but we respected each other. I loved him, but equally important, I liked him. That night I'd find out if he just thought of me as a kind and considerate friend, or whether I was something more to him.

The meal had almost finished cooking when my doorbell rang. I wiped my hands on a dish towel and opened the door for Samuel. He hadn't dressed up, which made sense; I mean, it wasn't like this was a date or anything. He had most likely come from the gym. He had sweatpants and a t-shirt on. His blond hair was still wet from a shower, and I thought he looked as good if not better than when he was in his stuffy lawyer suits.

"Mmm, something smells delicious. Did you make us chicken pot pie?"

"I sure did. I called your mother and got her recipe." I grinned.

"That's my favorite meal. I could kiss you."

Sparks ran down my spine. "Maybe later." I teased with a wink.

He chuckled.

"I just have to pull the pies out of the oven. You can pour the wine." He selected a bottle from the wine rack, took the corkscrew out of the drawer and went to the table.

I put the dessert in the oven so it would be ready when we were done. I served the pies and, if I say so myself, the crust looked perfect.

I watched Sam blow on a fork-full of the pie, then savor it in his mouth. He moaned in pleasure, and I felt the sound roll through me.

"It's amazing, just like my mother's chicken pot pie. You are too good to me."

"You deserve it. This is my way of thanking you for having my back with Mark and for helping Tessa for me."

He smiled at me. God, he was gorgeous. I felt my heart racing over what was going to happen after dessert. When we finished the pie, the stove timer went off with a ding. I pulled the cookie sheet out of the oven, grabbed the spatula, and headed to the table.

"Are those your famous chocolate chip cookies?"

I bobbed my head and smiled at the joy that spread across his face. "Resistance is futile."

He laughed. "Damn right it is. I'll take two, so we can save some for the movie."

"You're the best."

He took a bite and groaned. "You should sell these things. They're so good. I'm helping with the dishes, and I won't take no for an answer."

"If you insist." We carried the dishes to the kitchen, and I filled the sink with hot water and dish soap. I washed while Samuel dried. Each time our shoulders bumped, I felt my nerve endings tingle in anticipation of what would come next.

"So, you and Olivia looked pretty cozy out on the dance floor the other day. Is there something I should know?" He sounded hurt.

"Jealous?" I teased.

"Who, me? Why would I be jealous? It's not like you're—"

He hesitated to continue.

I took the opportunity to set the mood. "Siri, play 'All of Me' by John Legend, the hour loop." The song was special to me. It mirrored my friendship with Sam and my hopes of it becoming our love song.

Sam drew in a deep breath. "Why—?" His voice cracked.

"Why did I choose that song?"

He nodded.

I pressed my open hand against his heart, and I slowly stepped toward him. I kept up the pressure so he would step backward until he reached the refrigerator. I felt his heart pound at my nearness. His beautiful blue eyes looked vulnerable and spoke volumes. It felt like they begged me not to break his heart, or maybe that was what I was feeling. My pulse raced faster and faster. I prayed I was right, because if I wasn't, I could lose my best friend. The one person in my life that I trusted. The one I loved.

I cupped his cheek. "I chose this song because the entire time I danced to it, with Olivia, I wished it was you in my arms."

His tender gaze made me wonder if he could see into my soul. And whether it was tenderness for our friendship or more. I leaned in close. The sweet aroma of chocolate invaded my senses, making me hungry to taste it from his lips. I wrapped my hands around the back of his neck and gave him one sweet peck to see if he'd back out before I kissed him like a wild man. He didn't pull away. For the first time in my life, I felt butterflies in my stomach.

He grasped my butt with both hands and pressed our bodies together. A soft gasp of surprise and excitement escaped me. He took over and gave me slow, sensual kisses. Each one sent sparks of electricity through my veins.

I took back control and bombarded him with hungry passion.

His kisses turned possessive, and his blistering appetite set fire to my soul. We panted together to our love song.

He moaned into my mouth, and I rubbed his growing shaft. I poured everything I had into the kisses. I wanted him to feel my love. This moment had been a long time coming, and it was everything I had hoped for. I had to have more of him.

I opened my eyes, dropped to my knees and took his sweats and briefs to the floor with me. His erection bounced, and I whined in need to taste him.

"James," he growled.

It made me feel like I was the only man that mattered to him.

I caressed his thighs.

He groaned and reached down and pulled my t-shirt over my head.

I ran my tongue up both sides of his length. His clean soapy scent and taste had me pressing my butt cheeks together. I wanted him. Needed him. But there would be time for that later. Slowly, I took him into my mouth in sensual strokes up and down his member. Gradually I built up speed and pressure. I looked up and our eyes locked in a way that was incredibly erotic. I reached around and stimulated his anus with my fingers, letting him know what was yet to come. He put his head back and hissed.

I slowed my thrusts and softened the pressure of my tongue and breathed out to relax my muscles, allowing me to deep throat.

His body trembled. I brushed my other hand over his stomach and felt it tighten. He was close to coming.

I ran my hand down his thigh and reached for my throbbing cock. I continued to stroke his erection with my mouth and tongue while I worked myself into frenzied sensations of pleasure.

He reached down and took hold of both sides of my head and controlled my movements. It drove me crazy how into us he was.

Tingles grew in my groin and spread to my spine. With each stroke, the sensitivity increased, and I twitched.

"Don't stop." He demanded.

I wouldn't. I couldn't. I needed him to come first, but I was close now too. His excitement and the quivers of his hard, powerful body had me on edge. I looked up and his eyes rolled back, his eyelids shutting as blissful bursts of joy exploded into my throat. I released the pressure on his anus and he released me.

When he was spent, his body slid to the floor. He clamped his fist around mine. In no time, an electric buzz spread over me in waves. Muscle contractions rolled through my stomach, back, and chest. Spasms vibrated within my cock as I orgasmed into ecstasy. It was mind blowing.

Sam lay his head on my shoulder and wrapped his arms around me. "When I close my eyes at night, I think of you. I don't want you fixing me up with any more lame dates. I only want to love you for the rest of my life."

I choked up. It felt like a dream. All this time, he'd wanted me as much as I'd wanted him. He was my best friend and soul mate.

He sat up straight and gazed into my watery eyes. "Don't tell me the man that never stops talking has nothing to say in a moment like this?"

I swallowed hard, gave him a tender kiss and whispered, "I love you."

The End

Trust in Love
Gibby Campbell

Chapter One

No one was every going to mistake Brigid for a cis woman. She stood just over six feet tall, and that was without the heels. Her shoulders were broad, her voice was deep, and her hands were large with long fingers. That being said, she was beautiful. She had long, wavy brown hair and big green eyes that sparkled with humor.

By far Brigid's greatest feature, though, was her sunny disposition. She was raised in a small southern town where kindness and hospitality were seen as a way of life. The lesson had stuck, and now she could talk to anyone and make them feel welcome in less time than it took to pour a cup of coffee.

That southern town had taught her a lot, but not all of the lessons were good. The teasing started in the sixth grade and turned to bullying by the time she reached high school. Friends she had known her whole life suddenly started calling her names like faggot, he/she, and freak. When a boy beat her up on the bus, while the driver quietly looked on, her parents finally pulled her from the school.

Brigid remembered the day clearly. The pain and humiliation had faded over the years, but the indifferent look on the bus driver's face would stay with her forever. The man couldn't have cared less if she lived or died. It was one of the most gut-wrenching moments of her life, and it taught her a valuable lesson. It taught her the world was not always going to embrace or accept her.

At that point, Brigid had had a choice. She could conform and hide her true self, or she could fight for what she knew to be true. She chose the latter. It helped that she had the unwavering support and love of her parents. Many trans teens weren't as lucky. Some succumbed to the depression and shame and hid their true selves, while others committed suicide.

Brigid's parents knew the statistics and didn't want that to happen. They tried to understand and protect her, but it was difficult. When they finally dropped her at the airport four years later, there were some tears, but there was also a look of pure relief on both their faces.

That had been twelve years ago. Brigid still talked to her parents on a regular basis, and they occasionally came out for a visit, but she'd never been back to that southern town again. Instead, she'd put down roots in California and immersed herself in the San Diego LGBTQ community. They'd helped her find a job, a place to live, and a doctor who understood. The prescriptions helped change her body, and a visit to the courts changed her name. For the first time ever, she could live the life she was meant to live.

It wasn't always easy. The world was a dangerous place, and even as an adult Brigid encountered hatred. This took the form of insults, discrimination, and occasionally even some pushing and shoving. Ever the optimist, she shirked these encounters off and got on with her life.

That all changed the day her roommate, Kiki, was attacked.

Her trans friend had gone clubbing with a group of coworkers. When a migraine hit, she decided to leave early and walk to her car alone. Along the way she was approached by a group of drunken men. They hurled insults at her and pulled on her hair. Then the encounter became violent, and she was pummeled by fists and a bottle one was carrying. Fortunately, some bystanders intervened. Kiki was rushed to the hospital and spent two days in intensive care. The men were eventually caught and convicted, but this did nothing to heal Kiki. Her body was recovering, but her soul was completely shattered.

Brigid's was as well. That bubble of optimism she'd wrapped around herself evaporated, and she was left feeling just as lost and scared as she had in high school. She needed to slow down and find peace again, and she decided the best place to do that was in a small town.

After some serious research, she landed on Penny Lane. It was a little burg about an hour east of San Diego, and it too was LGTBQ friendly. It also happened to have a bakery for sale. Brigid and Kiki pooled their money and bought the bakery. The plan was to fix it up, turn it into a coffee shop, and live in the spacious apartment upstairs.

That had been a year ago, and the plan was working. Both women were slowly starting to breathe and let their guard down again. Brigid worked in the front of the store. She filled the orders and schmoozed the customers, while Kiki hid in the back and baked the pastries. Eventually, they started turning a profit, and they hired some staff and extended their business hours. Things were definitely looking up. Brigid reflected on this as she idly wiped the counter with a rag. Never in a million years would she have seen herself back in a small town, and yet here she was. What's more, it felt good. She looked through the door that led to the kitchen and saw Kiki bent over, meticulously decorating some petits fours. That made her smile. Then she looked out the front windows and saw the sun was just beginning to rise over the rooftops. They would be opening soon, but for now she could bask in the peace. She realized it felt a lot like hope.

Chapter Two

Two hours later, and the coffee shop was jumping. The regulars liked to get in before their jobs started, and Brigid greeted them like old friends. She took the orders and worked the register while the baristas, Mary and Deb, expertly made the drinks. The three kept up a lively banter as they worked, and they often involved the customers in their discussions.

Today they were debating if the Chargers had a shot at the playoffs. Mary was a huge fan, and she was detailing the merits of the team with enthusiasm.

Brigid couldn't resist teasing her. "Girl, you know they don't have a chance. The quarterback is easy on the eyes, but his aim isn't the greatest, and he tends to wander out of the pocket."

Mary started to argue, but Deb cut her off. She placed a mocha on the counter and asked, "So what are we talking about here? The quarterback's skill on the field, or in the bedroom?"

Everyone started to laugh, and Mary blushed. She was well into her sixties and a bit on the prim side. Then she shocked them all by saying, "He probably doesn't need perfect aim in the bedroom. That man is big, and well, you know, his thing probably is as well. He can wander a bit and still hit his mark." Then she winked.

The room erupted in laughter. Out of the corner of her eye, Brigid noticed the new guy had come in and was waiting his turn in line. He had an amused expression on his face and had clearly caught the entire conversation. Brigid felt her heart rate go up a beat.

The new guy had started coming in about a month ago, and word on the street was that he'd moved from Los Angeles for a job. He was tall, maybe an inch or two taller than Brigid, and he had a solid build. It was the kind that could engulf a girl in a big, sweet bear hug and make her feel all protected and safe. He also had expressive hands. She liked to imagine how they would feel running up and down her body. She guessed he was in his late thirties, as evidenced by the touch of gray in his hair, and he had the sweetest rear end she had ever seen.

Brigid nicknamed all her regular customers based on the drinks they ordered. When it was the new guy's turn, she greeted him with "Latte Extra Foam, how's it going?"

He grinned at her and replied, "Great. How are you?"

"Oh, you know, living the dream. Going with the usual today?"

He nodded. "Yes, and I think I'll try one of those bear claws too."

Brigid suppressed a smile as she bagged his order. The man had quite the sweet tooth, and he bought one of Kiki's desserts every morning with his coffee. She decided he must be a runner or something to burn off all that sugar, because he was one hot specimen of manhood. As he left with his order, she gave him another secret nickname. Hot Buns.

Brigid looked forward to seeing Hot Buns every morning, and the two started chatting more and more each time. She now knew he was an engineer for the city, an avid Rams fan, and single. She found the latter out one day when he was checking his emails and grunted.

"What's wrong? City got you working late again?" she asked.

He looked up and shook his head. There was a worry line on his forehead, and she suddenly had the urge to smooth it with her hand.

He gave her an exasperated look. "Just another friend wanting to fix me up on a blind date. The last one I went on was sheer torture."

She tutted sympathetically as she rang his order. "Well, it's nice to have friends who care, but I feel your pain. The last blind date I went on came up to about here on me," she gave him his change as she gestured toward her neck area with her other hand.

He laughed, and she noted his eyes lingered on her breasts. Before she could react, he had taken his change and pastry and moved down to wait for the latte. It was the first time he had checked her out, and once again, she felt her heart rate go up.

The next day Hot Buns was late. He got into the shop after the work crowd diminished, and he showed no inclination of leaving. He leaned against the counter, sipped his coffee, and tore off chunks of the chocolate croissant he ordered. While he ate, he chatted with Brigid about the upcoming Fourth of July celebration.

She was kneeling down stocking the pastries, and she laughed at his description of the mayor's float for the parade. As she stood up, she smoothed down her skirt and slid the display-case door shut. Only then did she notice him checking her out.

His eyes lingered on her size eleven wedge sandals. Then they slowly moved up her smooth legs, by far her most feminine feature, before taking in her perky C-cup breasts. His gaze finally came to rest on her eyes, and there was an odd expression on his face.

Brigid wondered if he had just clued into her trans status. If that was the case, he was rather dense, but she didn't have time to think about that now. She worried he might be a bigot, and she quickly sent Mary into the back room to distract Kiki. There was no way her friend could handle a nasty comment in her current state. It was better to be safe than sorry.

Her thoughts were interrupted when he spoke. "It was nice chatting with you, Brigid. You always make my day. By the way, my name's Brad, and you have the most beautiful smile I have ever seen." With that, he walked out of the store.

She watched him go with a bemused expression her face. She was hot and bothered for a good hour after he left.

Chapter Three

That weekend Brigid had some free time. The weather was gorgeous, and she decided to go fishing. As she packed her gear, she mused over the masculine hobby. Calling it a guy thing was sexist, but she couldn't help it. She had learned as a child with her father and his buddies. They had been big men who sucked on cigars and told inappropriate jokes as they waited for a bite. She had been disgusted by their behavior, but she still loved the atmosphere and the thrill of pulling fish from the water. It was one of the few interests she shared with her dad.

Brigid pulled into the city parking lot and pulled out her gear. The park was tiny, but it boasted a decent-sized pond that was regularly stocked with trout. She assessed the crowd as she walked down the path. There were a few old men fishing, a father with his young son, and a couple walking their dog.

A girl always had to be safe when out alone, but a trans woman had to be even more cautious. Brigid chose a spot close to the old men, but far enough away that they wouldn't strike up a conversation. She had just set the rods when she noticed a pick-up truck pull in. A big man got out with some gear and was making his way to her side of the pond. When he got closer, she realized it was Brad.

Brigid let out a sigh as she watched him approach. He appeared deep in thought and didn't seem to notice her. As he got closer, she could see the coffee cup he was holding. It had her store logo on it, and she realized the man had stopped there on his way to the park. Then she saw the pastry bag swinging in his other hand, tucked up under some fishing gear, and she started to laugh.

That's when he looked up and noticed her. He seemed surprised, but then his face broke out in a big smile.

"Hi, Brigid. What are you doing here?" Then he noticed her gear. "You like to fish?"

"Hi, Brad." She nodded at the coffee and teased, "I see you got your day off to a good start." Then she added, "Yah, I love to fish."

He stopped right in front of her and put his gear down. "A woman who loves to fish. I've been looking for a gal like you my whole life. Mind if I join you?"

She blinked in surprise. "Um, sure."

He quickly set up. "Any bites yet?"

"Nah, I just got here."

They sat down in their stadium chairs and stared out at the water in companionable silence. It was pretty with the sun glinting off the surface, and a slight wind was blowing through the trees. Then Brad quietly opened his bag and started eating the giant cookie inside. He politely offered her a piece, and she couldn't quite keep the smirk off her face when she declined.

"What's so funny?"

She answered with a question of her own. "How do you eat those treats every morning and not gain weight? Do you run?"

He shook his head around a mouthful of food. After he washed it down with some coffee he responded. "No. Running makes me want to cry. I hate all exercise, really, unless I'm playing a sport. Mostly I just have a high metabolism. It runs in the family."

"Lucky you. What types of sports do you play?"

He thought about it. "Anything with a racquet, I guess. I love tennis, racquetball, ping pong, pickle ball, I even played lacrosse in my younger years."

She looked amused. "Pickle ball?"

He nodded. "Yep. It's kind of like tennis, only you use a paddle and a plastic ball. It's a lot of fun."

She thought about it. "I might like that. I really like racquetball. There's something so satisfying about beating a blue ball all over the court." Then she blushed when she realized what she had said.

Now he was laughing loudly, and some of the old men looked over their way. In a more subdued voice he said, "Remind me to never play racquetball with you. But you really should try pickle ball. It's a blast. I could take you sometime."

She just looked at him but didn't respond.

Just then Brad got a bite and stood up to grab the rod. After he had reeled in the fish and released it, he sat back down. She was hoping he had forgotten his invitation in the commotion, but he hadn't.

"Seriously," he said, "I would like to take you out sometime. If not for pickle ball, then maybe on a proper date. We could get some dinner or go to a movie or something."

Brigid stared at him.

"You are so beautiful, and I am very attracted to you," he nervously added.

Now she was stunned. No straight man had ever said that to her before, and he was decidedly straight, not that she was an expert or anything. Then again, she realized he could be bi. She wasn't sure why she was trying to label him. She hated when people did that to her, and yet here she was doing the same thing to him.

Brad interrupted her thoughts. "I'm sorry. It's okay if you want to say no. I hope I haven't made you uncomfortable."

She realized he was embarrassed, as if she had rejected him. "Oh, no, Brad. It's not that. It's just, well, you *do* know what kind of girl I am, right?"

He nodded. "I have a pretty good idea, but maybe you can fill in some of the blanks."

Brigid was at a loss for words. She could feel her cheeks flaming, and she quickly slipped her hand into the pocket where she kept her mace. If this went bad, she was ready to run.

He must have seen her fear, as he ever-so-gently touched her face. "It's okay. I'm not a hater. I do have some questions, though. Is that all right?"

She sighed and slowly breathed in and out. "Fine. But please don't ask what my name used to be, or if I had surgery. Everyone asks that, and I just can't bear it."

He nodded. Then he traced one finger down her cheek and along her neck. "Hormones?" he quietly asked.

She nodded.

"Can't be easy," he murmured.

She nodded again.

Then he motioned toward her chest area. "Those are spectacular. Real?"

She beamed. "Well thank you. Yes. I had them done five years ago. Best money I ever spent."

He nodded, and the back of one hand slowly and gently brushed against a nipple before wandering down to curve around her waist. He leaned in. "I like how you feel next to me."

Brigid sighed and closed her eyes. She liked it too.

Then he nodded in her crotch area. "And what's going on down there?"

She gave him a sharp look. "I told you, no questions about surgery."

He sighed, "I kind of need to know what I'm getting into, but it's okay if you don't want to tell me." Then he slyly added, "I like to think I will find out sooner or later."

She pulled herself up tall and gave him a withering look. "You will not. I am a lady."

"I have no doubts. And I will treat you like a lady, as I am a gentleman."

Brigid sniffed the air. She was very attracted to him, and this was no time to be shy or embarrassed. If he truly was interested, and it looked like he was, then he had a right to know. She had come to terms with who she was years ago, and no hot and straight male was going to make her feel inferior. "I have the same thing going on as you do in your nether region, only mine is freshly shaved and tucked away" she finally said. Then she waited for his reaction.

Brad didn't bat an eye, but she could tell he was thinking hard on things. Then he shook his head in wonder. "A girl with a dick," was all he said.

She bristled a bit and continued to wait for the inevitable retreat. Instead, he gently touched her hand. "I am very attracted to you. You make my day every morning with your uplifted spirit and that beautiful smile of yours. I would like to take you out on a date."

Brigid was beyond shocked. She shifted in her seat, "I am flattered, Brad, I truly am. But I suspect you have never been with a trans girl before. I'm not sure you could handle it, not to mention all the people in your social circle. I *know* some of them won't be able to handle it. And I am done having relationships in secret."

He thought some more. "Well, you're right. I've never been with— what did you call it?—a trans girl before. I have banged plenty of female rear ends, though. Seems to me this is not much different. I'm thinking of all kinds of things you could do to me, and I could do to you."

Her mouth fell open into a small O.

Then his hand boldly rested on her leg, and his thumb gently stroked her inner thigh along the seam of her shorts.

Brigid was so turned on, she swore she would cum right there. God, it had been so long, but she truly was a lady, and she wanted a relationship and not a quick fling. She pushed his hand away. "I'm available tomorrow night for a date and nothing more, if you're interested."

He grinned. I'll pick you up at six. Where do you live?

"Right above the coffee shop." She gave her number. "Just text me, and I'll come down." No way she could bring him into the apartment. Kekes would freak out.

He plugged her number into his phone, and then the two continued to fish for over two hours. It was obvious they got along well together, and Brigid was looking forward to their date.

Chapter Four

It went better than expected. Brad showed up right on time and was a true gentleman. He opened her door and made sure she was sitting comfortably before driving to the restaurant. They talked through the entire meal. She learned all about his civil engineering job and found it fascinating. Then she told him about her business. She had him in stitches when she described the day the coffee machine went berserk and splattered hot water everywhere.

Brad was a great listener. He rested his chin on top of his folded hands and asked relevant questions to keep the conversation going. Every now and then he would reach out and touch her arm or hand, and his eyes twinkled as she talked. It made her feel important and interesting. It had been a long time since Brigid had clicked this well with a man, and it felt good.

Their next date was two days later. This time Brad took her to an outdoor concert, as they had discovered a shared love of alternative rock. The band was being touted as San Diego's next big thing. Ten minutes into the concert, Brad quietly handed her a pair of earplugs. The music was that bad. Brigid burst out laughing, and that's when he leaned down and kissed her for the first time.

After that, the dates kept coming faster and faster. The two went to galleries, took long walks in the park, and even played a few rounds of pickle ball. Brad easily beat her in that sport, but she held her own in racquetball. Finally, after three months, the two had settled into an easy relationship. There had been plenty of cuddling and make-out sessions along the way, and Brigid was slowly falling in love. Now Brad was gently pressing her to take things further, but she still put him off.

She discussed it with Kiki while getting ready for a date. "It's going so well, but I still haven't met his family or friends."

"And you are worried he's ashamed?" said her friend. Then she added, "Plus, you're worried straight boy won't be able to handle things between the sheets."

"Well, yah. You know how bad that could go."

Kiki gave her a wistful smile. "Or it could turn out great." She handed Brigid the bottle of hair spray. "The poor man is probably all blue-balled and dying for it at this point. You can't keep stringing him along."

"I know." Brigid ran her fingers through her roots and misted them with the spray. "It's just, I really like him, you know?"

Kiki gave her a sad look. "Yah, I know. But you have to talk to him about this. The longer you drag it out, the worse it will be for both of you."

Brigid nodded as she critically eyed herself in the mirror. Then she dusted a bit more powder on her nose before standing up. She hugged her friend and sighed, "Okay. I'm going to do it. I'm going to talk to him tonight."

"Good. Call me if you need me, and good luck."

***

Brad waited until they had finished eating dinner and were curled up on the couch watching a movie. Then he asked, "Are you going to tell me what's bothering you, babe?"

Brigid sat up straight and edged away from him ever-so-slightly. "How did you know something was bothering me?"

He laughed, "You've been a squirmy-wormy all night long. Something's definitely on your mind. Talk to me."

She sighed and stared at her hands. Then she looked over and quietly asked, "How come I've never met any of your family or friends? Are you ashamed of me?" She could feel her breathing pick up.

Brad looked at her in surprise. "What? Of course, I'm not ashamed of you."

"Then why haven't I met anyone?" Now tears were welling in her eyes.

He leaned over and kissed each eyelid. "I've been putting it off because I'm ashamed of *them*, not you. My family, in particular, are going to be real asshats about all of this."

She couldn't help it and laughed. "Asshats? You're such an old man sometimes."

He tweaked her nose. "Not an old man. A gentleman. I don't want to swear in front of you." Then he leaned back against the cushions and stared off in the distance. Finally, he looked back at her. "I guess I can see where you're coming from on meeting everyone. I've certainly met most of your friends. I do have a family event coming up next weekend. It's about an hour away from here. You want to come?"

This was big. If he was willing to introduce her to his family, then he was in it for the long term. But if it went bad, it could end what they had.

Finally, she answered, "I will go on two conditions."

"Do tell," was the dry response.

"I drive separately, in case I need to make a quick exit, and you tell them ahead of time about me. I won't be held responsible for, I don't know, killing your grandma or something."

He laughed. "Done."

***

Brigid was so nervous. She changed her dress five times and agonized over what gift to bring Brad's mom. She finally settled on a good bottle of wine and a simple bouquet of flowers.

When she pulled in at the house, Brad was already there waiting. He immediately got out of his car and jogged over to open her door.

"You nervous?"

"God, yes," she grimaced.

He laughed. "Me too. Here goes nothing."

They braced themselves and headed in.

Neither should have worried. Brad's family couldn't have been more gracious. His mom greeted Brigid with a hug, and his dad smiled and shook her hand. She was introduced to three sisters, one brother, several aunts and uncles, and way too many cousins to count.

Best of all, though, was Brad's grandma. She was a sassy eighty years old with a great sense of humor and a quick wit. It was obvious she adored her family and liked to tease them. She included Brigid in the fun by making comments about her sanity for falling for "the likes of Bradley."

Things were going so well that Brigid started to relax. She noticed some of his family quietly checking her out, but that was nothing new, and no one was acting uncomfortable. They were there to celebrate a cousin's birthday, and a lot of the adults were drinking. This made everyone relax even more.

Grandma, in particular, was getting tipsy. Toward the end of the evening she leaned over to Brigid and conspiratorially asked, "I'm curious, where do you hide your wiener, dear? Assuming you still have one, that is." She ignored the gasps in the room and continued, "Do you tuck your balls inside? I hear some people can do that."

The entire room cringed, and several people cried out, "Grandma!"

Brad ran over and was looking angry, but Brigid waved him off. She knew the old lady was just being curious, and she also knew how to calm the situation down with some good old-fashioned southern charm. She smiled and mischievously replied, "Oh, honey, a lady never tells. But I will say this. It all depends on how tight the pants are." Then she winked.

The entire room burst out laughing, and just like that, the tense moment had passed.

Brad just shook his head in amazement.

They left shortly after. As he walked her to her car, he asked, "You coming back to my place?" She could see the obvious lust in his eyes.

"God, yes."

He followed her the whole way home.

Chapter Five

It took under an hour to get to his place. They started kissing in the foyer and staggered down the hallway as clothes were coming off. Brad, ever the dorky gentleman, picked her up at the bedroom door and carried her to the bed.

Brigid howled with laughter, but then she put a steadying hand on his chest. "I'm going to go freshen up. Why don't you get into bed, and I'll come join you in a minute?"

He nodded, and she could see him eagerly shirking off the rest of his clothes as she stepped into the bathroom.

Brigid stood with her back leaning up against the door. She willed herself to breathe in and out slowly as she stared at her reflection in the mirror. Her lipstick was smeared, and her hair was askew, but mostly she noticed her eyes. They were wide, wild, and showed a primal fear, just like that of a cornered animal.

Brigid had never really been comfortable with sex. She rarely had an orgasm, and when she was in bed with a man, she mostly just focused on pleasing him and finding a connection. But Brad was different. He was the kind of guy that would make it all about her, and the thought was terrifying.

For one thing, he had only ever been with cis women. How was he going to handle her body? She finished unbuttoning her dress and let it slide to the floor. Then she eased out of her stockings so she was left standing in just a bralette and pair of panties. They were both pretty, with lace and satin around the edges, but she still felt self-conscious.

To ease her anxiety, she grabbed a tissue and fixed her makeup. Then she tidied her hair, rinsed her mouth with water, and smiled at the mirror. She told herself she would be confident and brave and continued to breathe deeply to calm down. When she finally stepped out of the bathroom, her head was held high, and her hands were at her side. Let him take it all in.

Brad was propped up against some pillows with his naked chest showing above the blanket. He had one light on by the bed, and it cast a soft glow over Brigid. His eyes wandered all over her body with a look of pure appreciation on his face. "You are so beautiful," he said, as he motioned her with his hand to come join him.

She glowed at the praise and crawled into bed to snuggle up against him. Brad wrapped his big arms around her and just held her. Then he gently started kissing her, as his hands wandered up to her chest and started playing with her breasts.

It felt so damn good. Brigid was losing herself in the moment. Her bra had come off and now one of his hands started to wander down toward her legs. That brought her back to reality in a hurry. She pushed away from him, and sighed. She could see his rock-hard erection poking out from under the blanket. But before she went there, they needed to talk.

"I have a few ground rules, Brad."

He grinned with a flushed face. "Okay, baby. Anything you want."

She smiled. He really was adorable. Then she reached down and pulled off her panties. Brad followed the movement with his eyes, and he had an aroused expression on his face.

She touched her genitals. "Think of this as a much softer and thinner version of yours. It requires a gentler touch." Then she stroked her frenulum. "This is where I like being touched the most, but again, you have to be gentle."

He nodded, and his fingertips gently started stroking her shaft.

Brigid ran her hands over his chest and down his arms. She sighed deeply before pulling away again. "More rules."

Brad laughed. "Lay 'em on me."

"Okay, first, don't ever call mine a dick or penis. I like to think of it more as a really large clitoris."

Brad started stroking her frenulum again and mumbled, "Clit. Got it."

"I don't like receiving oral, but I love giving it, which is what I plan to do to you tonight."

Brad moaned, "Yessss..."

She laughed. "The opposite holds true for anal. I can take all the stick you want to give me back there, but I doubt I'll ever return the favor, except maybe with my finger. And it's completely off the table tonight. I like to have things clean, plus we're going to need lube, and I doubt you have the kind I like to use."

Now Brad was shaking his head. "My little bossy girl. Any more rules before I share mine?"

She raised her eyebrows. "You have rules?"

"Yes, but please continue, ladies first."

"Oh, that's it for me, honey. Do tell. What are your rules?"

"I always want you to feel safe with me," he said seriously. "I don't ever want to hurt you or make you feel uncomfortable. Since I'm new to all of this, you're going to have to speak up and tell me when things aren't right."

She nodded.

"You sure, Brig? Because you're not always forthcoming with the communication."

She leaned over and kissed him. "I promise I'll speak up. Any other rules?"

"Yes. Just one. I will always take care of your needs before I get to my own."

She bit her lip. "Oh, Brad, that is so sweet. But the thing is, I don't often have an orgasm. The hormones have messed that up a bit. I don't even masturbate. I mostly get off just being close to you."

He had a determined look on his face. "We'll see about that." Then they were done talking, as their bodies were speaking a different kind of language.

When they were done, Brad spooned her and whispered, "I had no idea it could be that good." He had not given her an orgasm, but the connection they felt to one another was overpowering. Brigid smiled in the dark.

As they drifted off to sleep, she realized something. In that moment she felt what most cis women must feel all the time when thoroughly loved and accepted by their man. She fell asleep in wonder.

Chapter Six

Three months went by, and the relationship deepened even further. The two had a blast exploring each other's bodies, and along the way they figured out how to bring Brigid to orgasm. More importantly, the two had fallen in love.

Brigid had met a few of his friends before, but tonight she was meeting the rest of them. Brad was taking her to a New Year's Eve party. Well, that was his intent. As usual, she insisted on driving separately.

He was not happy. "When are you going to trust me? Trust what we have? Most of them already know. They've seen the social media posts, and they have been asking to meet you."

She sighed. Trust wasn't something trans people gave freely. It had to be earned, after a long time, and they just weren't there yet. To him, she simply said, "I'll feel better driving separately."

He begrudgingly agreed, and they headed out to the party.

It was in a small warehouse on the edge of town. The building had been decorated with vintage string lights weaving through the rafters, and a makeshift stage had been set up for a band. There was a bar along one side, tables along the other, and a hallway in the back that led to a makeshift coat room and the restrooms.

Brad kept her by his side and took her around to meet everyone he knew. He had a lot of friends, and there were even a few of his coworkers at the party. Everyone was super friendly, and they joked about finally meeting her. She could feel their curious gaze on her body, but she was used to that, and she was enjoying the attention of some of his female friends. They bombarded her with questions on how she managed the smoky eye look, and several complimented her on her purse and shoes.

Brigid was starting to feel comfortable and eventually left Brad's arm. She was social by nature, and she was having a great time mingling with the crowd. It was tough to hear people over the band, though, and she kept having to drink more water to soothe her hoarse throat.

Eventually, she had to excuse herself to go use the restroom. She made her way down the hallway and was just pushing in the ladies door, when a man stopped her. It was Stuart, one of Brad's friends. He grabbed her arm and gave her a disgusted look.

"You're going in the wrong one, dude."

Brigid blinked and pulled her arm away. She tried to turn around and head back to the party, but he followed behind and ranted at her.

"What kind of a sick freak are you, anyway? We all think you're brainwashing Brad, and you're going to go to hell for this. God doesn't like freaks like you."

Brigid stopped in her tracks. She didn't want the rest of the group to hear them, as it would embarrass Brad, so she just stood there and took it. The nasty man droned on and on, and she could feel one tear slip out and trail down her cheek. She was also feeling sick to her stomach and clutched her belly.

The moment seemed to go on forever, but suddenly Brad was standing between her and the jerk. He shoved Stuart hard against the wall and then turned to hug Brigid. "Are you okay, baby? What did he say to you?"

She wiped her face. "Nothing I haven't heard before. I'm sorry. I'm not feeling so good. I think I'm going to leave, okay? I'll call you later."

Brad tried to stop her, but then Stuart snuck up and punched him from behind. Brad whirled around to deal with him, and that gave Brigid the chance she needed to flee. She ran to her car, slipping on the gravel walkway, and peeled out of the parking lot as the tears started to flow more freely.

Meanwhile, Brad was trying to deal with Stuart. He wanted to just walk away, but the idiot wouldn't let it go. He was drunkenly shouting out Bible verses as he followed Brad down the hall. Finally, Brad turned around and punched Stuart in the gut, and the jerk dropped to the ground like a sack of potatoes.

Brad frantically looked around the room, but he couldn't find Brigid. A crowd had gathered and was staring at him. That's when he really lost his cool.

He yelled, "This is who I am. This is the relationship I'm in, and it's for the long haul. Like it or leave it, but tell me now so I don't have to be careful around those of you who are going to be assholes. I don't fucking ever want to put Brig through this again." Now his hands were on his legs as he tried to catch his breath.

A woman walked up and hugged him. "She's a sweetheart, Brad. Go for it."

Others in the room nodded.

Then a coworker teased, "She's super-hot and way out of your league. But chill. No one cares and no one is judging. Stuart is a dick and a drunk, and we all know it."

Another yelled, "Yah, man. Good job shutting that asshole up."

Brad couldn't help it and started laughing.

"You better go get your girl," another called out. "She looked pretty upset when she left."

Brad nodded and headed for the exit.

Chapter Seven

It took Brad ten minutes to get to Brigid's apartment. Kiki let him in, gave him a look of encouragement, and then quickly excused herself.

Brigid was sitting on the couch. There were tissues strewn all around her, and mascara was running down her face.

He went and kneeled in front of her. "I'm sorry, baby. I got it all straightened out. Are you okay? Did he hurt you? I wish you hadn't left like that." His voice sounded anxious.

She wiped her eyes and sputtered, "No, he didn't even touch me. He was just spewing hatred. I had to get out of there. I'm sorry I left, but I felt so awful. He made me feel like I'm ruining your life. I never wanted this for you."

"What are you talking about? The only thing you've done for my life is make it complete, Brig. I love you. I want to spend the rest of my life with you. That's what I told them, if you had stuck around to hear it. When are you going to stop running and learn to trust me?"

She calmed herself. "You don't understand. I know what this is like. What it's going to be like for you if you stay with me. The judgements. The hatred. The feeling you're less than or a freak in the eyes of society. You know how many friends I have lost to suicide? I don't want any of that for you. I never did. But the attraction was just so strong…" Her voice trailed off.

"I'm trying to understand, Brig. But you never want to talk about this stuff."

She sighed. "What would be the point?" Then she threw her hands in the air, "What's the point of any of this, really?"

"What are you saying?"

"I'm saying we should break up."

Now he was furious. "Don't I get a say in this? You think so little of me that you think I can't handle this?"

She gave him a weak smile. "You're a big, strong man, Brad, but even you can't fight off the hatred. It can get violent. Lord knows I've been there, and Kekes even worse than me. I know you think you can protect us, but what happens when there's a whole group of them? When you're not invited to events because of me? When your job fires you because of me?"

"Jesus, Brig. It's never going to get that bad. This is the twenty-first century. But if it does, we fight. Hell, we can take self-defense classes together, get some mace, I don't know, something. The world is changing. It's getting better. Gay people are able to do so much more than they ever have before. Why not trans people as well?"

She just stared at him. She understood. She really did. She had hope for the world as well. But she was getting tired, and she didn't want to see him hurt like so many others she had loved.

Brad pulled her into his arms and hugged her, and that made her start crying all over again.

"Oh, baby. Please stop crying. What do you want, Brig? Talk to me. I'll do anything to make you feel better."

She wailed, "I want to be free to *live*. I want to be the person inside of me without having to worry how it affects those outside of me... how it affects you. I want to be the woman I was born to be without hiding or being ashamed."

He shook his head in amazement. "You are, baby. That's what I see. The beautiful, messy, fun-loving, outgoing woman who is true to herself and so damn lovable I sometimes have to pinch myself to know what we have is real."

She gave him an anguished smile. "That's just it. I'm not real. The world is never going to believe I'm a girl, Brad. Please just leave. It's better if you do."

He stared at her for a long moment. Then he stood up and quietly left the apartment. The door clicking behind him sounded so final. Brigid covered her face and wailed.

Chapter Eight

Kiki immediately came out of her bedroom and tried to comfort her friend. Once Brigid had calmed down, she yelled at her. "You're throwing it all away. This is what we live for. He's giving you unconditional love. Why would you give up on that?"

Brigid looked at her in shock and then anger. "You're one to talk. It's New Year's Eve, and you're hiding at home. You're too afraid to even go out in public anymore."

Kiki stomped into her room, no small task in three-inch stilettos, and came back out with a brochure. She shoved it under Brigid's nose.

"What's this?"

"The line dancing group I joined four months ago. Ever since you and Brad-babe got serious. You inspired me to try again, Brig. You gave me hope."

Brigid stared at the brochure. "This looks so lame… oh my god… but so much fun."

"Right? Picture it. A roomful of people and yours truly stomping around, off tempo and all gangly arms and legs flying about. It's the most friggin' fun I've had in years. And they are all so kind and welcoming to me. We meet for book discussions, mani-pedis. God help me, I even went bowling last week."

Brigid gave her a misty smile. "I'm so happy for you, girl. You're finally healing."

Kiki came over and wiped her face with a tissue. "Baby steps. That's all we can do. Take baby steps. You need to do your own bit of healing. You also need to clean up this godawful mug and go get your man."

"I don't know if I can, Kekes."

"Sure you can. All you need to do is take a leap of faith. Life isn't worth living unless you're taking risks. My dipshit daddy gave me those words of advice. One of the few good things he ever did give me."

Brigid laughed. "Well, that, and those narrow shoulders. What I wouldn't give for those."

Kiki laughed and kissed her forehead. "Come on. Let's get you cleaned up. Then you have some talking to do with your man."

***

Brigid flew out of the apartment fifteen minutes later. If she knew Brad, he would be at his house pacing. She headed toward her car but then stopped short. Brad was in the parking lot. His head was down, and sure enough, he was pacing.

He stopped when he saw her, and they stared at each other.

He finally spoke. "I couldn't leave you."

She sighed. "I apparently can't leave you either." Then she ran straight at him and into his arms. They hugged and kissed.

Brad finally pulled away. "We need to talk about all of this, Brig."

She nodded, took his hand, and led him to the coffee shop. She unlocked the door, switched on the lights, and then started the coffee maker. While it brewed, she opened the dessert case and put two lemon poppy seed muffins on a plate. Then she set the plate on the table and sat down across from him. He immediately broke off a piece of the muffin and started eating. That made Brigid smile.

Brad waited until they both had a steaming cup of coffee in front of them. Then he squeezed her hand and simply said, "Tell me."

She did. She started with her childhood and the first glimmers she had that she might be a girl, how her parents treated her, how her friends treated her, and on and on. She took him right up to the present day and filled in a lot of the blanks he had. Brad was aware that Kiki had been attacked, but he had never known the details until now. It was a lot to take in, and he could feel his gut clenching.

When Brigid finally finished, it was four in the morning, and both of them were emotionally and physically exhausted. He had no idea what to say, so instead he pulled her into his arms and just cradled her. They sat like that for quite some time, and then finally pulled apart.

"I can't fix any of your old hurts," Brad said. "And I know I can't always protect you, or us, from what might come in the future. But that doesn't mean we shouldn't be together. I love you, and I know how much you love me. We have to trust in that, Brig. We have to try. We have to work to make that enough, even if the rest of the world doesn't like it."

She nodded. "I do trust us. I'm just now beginning to realize that."

He smiled. "And just think, when our kids are adults, the world will be even better than it is now."

She gave him a look. "Kids? Really? You would be up for adoption?"

He laughed. "Sure. I guess now is a good time as any to tell you I was adopted."

She shook her head. "Seems I wasn't the only one keeping secrets."

"No more of that," he admonished. "From now one we talk and tell each other everything. And never again will there be a mention of breaking up."

She tried to respond, to agree, but he had already covered her mouth with his lips.

Who knew what the future held? But Brigid decided, with Brad by her side, it would be fun to find out together.

It was true, trans people did not trust easily, but when they finally gave it, the bond was everlasting.

The End

Her Rogue Identity
Patricia Elliott

Dedicated to all who feel different.

Chapter One

It had happened again.

Was it ever going to end?

Ashlynn Jacobs knew she wasn't as beautiful as the average woman, but did she really look so much like a guy that strangers had to debate it amongst themselves on the bus? In front of other people, no less, and looking directly at her?

When the bus stopped, she grabbed her backpack and made a mad dash for the door. It didn't matter that she was a few miles away from her destination. She'd rather walk than subject herself to more of their barbs. Ones that dug deep into her heart, spreading across her psyche.

Ashlynn adjusted her backpack on her back, then pulled on the hood of her sweater. Dark clouds loomed overhead. But she put her sunglasses on anyway, preferring to hide as much of her face as she could. Shuffling her feet as she walked, she ducked her head and stuffed her hands in her pockets, trying to hide her flushed cheeks.

At nineteen, she thought she'd have had this whole identity thing figured out and be comfortable in her own skin. She had wide lineback shoulders, small breasts, and a face that was a cross between a boy's and a girl's. If she cut her hair short, she could pass as a boy, which meant all the cute, short haircuts were out of the picture. That thought and more kept her mind a confusing mess.

She didn't like things that most girls liked—make-up, perfume, dresses. Not that she could rock a dress with her body type anyway, but still, shouldn't she like those things? She was more interested in martial arts and hockey than anything else. Being out on the ice was the one place she felt free, free to be herself. You couldn't really see what anyone looked like under all that gear, and it felt like a whole other world. She didn't have to deal with the jeers of strangers.

Sometimes she wished she could become a hermit and never have to deal with another living soul. But then, she would miss Justin and Jessie Harris, twins she had been friends with since elementary school. They treated her like a sister. And then there was Wesley, their older brother. She'd caught him watching her with curiosity now and then. She couldn't help but wonder if he thought the same way about her as everyone else seemed to. He never said much, but he gave off a weird aura, and it made her insides antsy.

As she walked by the park, a kid yelled, "Heads up."

She looked up in time to see a football racing towards her head, and the next thing she knew, she was sprawled on the ground, sporting a nasty headache.

"Are you okay, mister?" the pre-teen boy asked, looking at her with concern as he picked up the ball.

"Yes, I'm fine," she snapped at him. "Just get out of here."

"Sorry for hitting you with the ball."

"Ya, whatever."

"Come on, Luke, leave the grouch alone," another boy said, pulling his friend back to the grassy field.

Ashlynn knew she should be grateful for his concern, but she just didn't have it in her. Not today. Rolling over onto her knees, she gingerly touched her cheek. A lump was already forming. It was beginning to feel like she should have stayed in bed.

Standing up, Ashlynn pulled her phone out of her pocket and messaged Jessie to let her know she wouldn't be much longer. She was at 144th Street now, and her friends lived on one 142nd. They were heading to the movies, and Wesley was driving because their parents were out of town. He was the only one that had his license.

He had offered to pick her up, and she'd almost taken him up on it, but her stepdad, Carl, would have given him the third degree. They hadn't met each other yet, and Carl thought everyone was doing the nasty and would have threatened him with his one and only shotgun. And given that Wes was five years older than she was, her stepdad would probably shoot first and ask questions later. She loved that he was so protective of her and her mom, but it drove her crazy.

Ashlynn walked up to the door of her friends' house and knocked. The door swung open and there stood a blue-eyed, blond-haired Wes with a mouth-watering bare chest. Her eyes followed his perfect abs until a pair of snug blue jeans got in the way.

"Hey, squirt," he said, his voice echoing through her senses.

She swallowed hard and squeaked a hello before rushing by him and barging into Jessie's bedroom.

Her friend spun around with a shriek, wearing only a pink bra and matching undies. "Geez, Ash, you almost gave me a heart attack," she said before turning back to face her closet. "I can't find anything to wear."

Ashlynn leaned down and picked through the articles of clothing that were in a heap on the floor, like they'd been plucked off the hangers and dropped in disgust. "They're all cute. What's the problem?"

Jessie ran a hand through her long blonde hair. "I don't want cute. I want sexy. I need sexy."

"You have looked at yourself in the mirror, right? Besides, it's not like you're going on a date."

Her friend just wanted to look good for the guy working at the ticket booth. But in Ashlynn's opinion, Jessie didn't have to work hard to knock the socks off someone she was interested in. Jessie, Justin, and Wes all looked like they could be runway models. A sharp contrast to what Ashlynn herself looked like. She'd always envied Jessie, and even her vagina found her friend attractive. But that was mostly because of the games they'd played with each other throughout their teen years, learning how to orgasm with each other's help.

"I'd die to look like you," Ashlynn said, picking up a cute pair of blue shorts and a tank top that said Beautiful Disaster. "Just wear this."

Jessie shook her head, but then pointed at her. "I think you'd look perfect in that, though."

"Uh uh. No way. I'd be the laughingstock of the theatre if I wore that. I'm perfectly happy in my oversized sweater."

There was no way she'd broadcast her nearly flat chest to the world. It was like every other woman in the world had breasts and she'd drawn the short straw, leaving her somewhere in between a woman and a man. Heck, she even had a few stray strands of hair on her chest, between her breasts. She shaved them, of course, but they drove her nuts.

"Come on, let's knock the world dead tonight," Jessie encouraged.

"The only way I'd knock the world dead is by actually killing them, and then where would I be?" Ashlynn answered, smirking.

Jessie walked over to her, in her semi-nakedness, and framed Ashlynn's face between her palms, giving her a gentle kiss on the lips before resting her forehead against hers. "Don't do that. Don't knock yourself down."

Ashlynn shrugged. "I'm just accepting what is."

Jessie tugged her towards a full-length mirror. "What do you see?"

Ashlynn's light brown hair was a straggly mess from having been underneath the hoody, and a purplish-brown bruise was forming on her cheek from where the football had hit her. "I look like I've gone three rounds with Mike Tyson."

"You know what I see?" Jessie said, running her hands down Ashlynn's arms. "I see a beautiful, gorgeous woman, with eyes as deep and intense as the ocean. Someone that I would die for."

"I do too, but it's definitely not me."

"Say I'm beautiful."

"You're beautiful."

"No, you dork." Jessie laughed. "I want you to tell yourself you're beautiful. Do it for me, okay?"

"I'm beautiful," Ashlynn muttered, looking down at the ground.

Jessie slapped her on the butt. "Be good and say it like you believe it."

Ashlynn's core tingled at the contact, especially because she hadn't had a good orgasm in days and her best friend was behind her, almost naked. They'd been so busy lately that they hadn't played around as much as they used to. But after her experience today, she craved intimacy… needed it. And it meant the world to her that someone wanted her when no one else did.

"Jessie."

"I know," her friend whispered, slipping her hand between Ashlynn's thighs and cupping her mound, pressing lightly.

Ashlynn's underwear grew damp with anticipation. She turned in her friend's arms and led her backward towards the bed when a knock sounded at the door.

"You girls ready yet? We're going to be late," Justin stated.

They touched foreheads and giggled, then stepped back from each other.

"Boys," Jessie said, rolling her eyes as she turned to pick an outfit.

They were going to watch a new mutant movie, one that was all the rage in the box office. For as long as Ashlynn could remember, she loved the idea of having superpowers and naturally gravitated towards movies that had mutants. Jessie would rather see a romance, but since the boys were tagging along, it had to be man-friendly too. If they went to a romance movie, they wouldn't get enough peace to watch it. The boys would spend the whole time joking about how corny it was.

When the girls stepped into the living room, Wes looked up and locked eyes with Ashlynn, as though he were studying her. Then a knowing grin spread across his face, like he knew they'd been up to something naughty in the bedroom. Embarrassment stirred in her as she tore her eyes away from his. Their exchange had her hoping she could sit between Jessie and Justin, away from Wesley. The vibe he gave off made her nervous.

"Just give me a minute, and we'll be ready to go," Jessie said as she disappeared down the hallway and into the kitchen.

Not long later, she reappeared with a pink leather jacket to go with her hot pink skirt, and they all piled into Wesley's big-wheeled four-by-four. She and Jessie slipped into the backseat while the boys sat in the front. Ashlynn didn't have her license yet, but she often wondered what car she'd buy if she found the courage to do her road test.

Leaning back, she rested her elbow on the armrest and stared out the window. It was nine at night but the sun was still shining, as it was early summer and it didn't set until later. They had just graduated from high school, and Ashlynn was beyond grateful. She no longer had to endure the stares of her classmates, the whispers behind her back, or the crooked grins from the boys as they dared each other to ask her out.

It was one of the reasons she hadn't been on a date yet. If someone asked her, she couldn't tell if they were being genuine or playing a prank on her. Sometimes she wished she could be more like Jessie. She had all the boys falling over her, and you could easily tell that they liked her. Even the acting and modeling world was vying for her. It was why Jessie had her entire future planned out, right until she dropped dead.

And here Ashlynn was, without a clue as to what she wanted to do with her life beyond simply waking up the next day.

"Earth to Ashlynn," Wes said, glancing at her in the rearview mirror.

"Huh, what?" she asked, dragging her gaze to meet his.

"We're here."

"Oh."

"Were you dreaming about anyone in particular?" Wes asked, with that dreamy ass grin of his.

Ashlynn rolled her eyes. "As if anyone has given me anything to dream about."

"Come on, guys," Justin said. "We're going to be late."

They had about fifteen minutes left before the actual movie started, but they knew Justin didn't want to miss the movie trailers. Wesley jumped out of the car, and Ashlynn opened her door to climb down. He held out his hand, and she took it. She swallowed hard as electricity sizzled between their fingers, like when you rub your feet on the carpet and then touch the person closest to you.

"Thanks," she muttered, as she snatched her hand away the minute she could. It was pointless to feel like this about a boy. They never returned the feeling, so it was best never to start and to ignore it. Ashlynn took a step back and created some distance between them. The less contact the better.

The only one she trusted was Jessie, but even then, she knew there was no future with her either. They were just friends. And that was okay. But she knew that when the time came to let her go, like if Jessie ever got married, her world would be a lonely place.

She trailed after her friends as they walked towards the theatre, watching them interact with each other. Wes and Justin flanked Jessie protectively, and it brought a smile to Ashlynn's face. They loved their sister and would do anything to protect her, and she them. Sadly, Ashlynn had no siblings and was in awe of their close relationship with each other.

She only had her mom and stepdad, but they went out of town a few days ago for work, so it was just her at the moment. It was kind of lonely, but she liked the freedom of doing what she wanted when she wanted, like being out later than her usual curfew.

"Are we going dutch?" Ashlynn asked when they reached the ticket booth.

Wes pulled out four tickets from his pocket. "I got us covered."

After stopping by the concession stand and getting popcorn, they climbed into their seats with only seconds to spare as the final trailer ended. Because of the rush and not wanting to miss anything, Ashlynn found herself sitting between Justin and Wesley. *Joy.* She was stuck between two testosterone-filled males. She brought her straw to her lips and took a sip, trying to ignore that specific fact.

Wes leaned over, his lips awfully close to her ear. "I guess you're my date tonight."

The drink went down the wrong pipe, and Ashlynn started hacking up a storm. Leaning over, she tried to get her breath back.

"Is she okay?" Jessie asked, peering around Justin to look at her.

"I'll be f-fine." Ashlynn said, continuing to cough as she hit her chest a few times, casting a side glance at Wesley, who had settled back in his seat with a grin. Oh, she wanted to smack him so badly. In fact, she was going to do just that. Turning, she slugged him in the shoulder, making him laugh.

"Hey, can you guys keep it down?" someone said from a few rows back. "The movie is starting."

"Ya, keep it down," Wes whispered to her.

"Shut up," Ashlynn grumbled, hitting his shoulder again for good measure.

This time, he grabbed her hand and brought it down to the armrest, not letting it go. She tried to pull out of his grip, but he just tightened it more.

"You hit me, so this is your punishment."

Rather than fight and draw attention to herself, Ash stuck her tongue out at him and slid further down in her seat. Her hand tingled as his thumb caressed the sensitive spot between her thumb and index finger, making her shiver with awareness. Did he notice? She didn't dare look at him in case he did. She wasn't ready for whatever look would be in his eyes, whether mockery or heat.

There was a tap on Ashlynn's shoulder, and she looked over to see Jessie gesturing at their conjoined hands, a wide grin on her face. "You go, girl," she mouthed.

Ashlynn shook her head. She had no plans on going anywhere with Wesley, even if her body was revving its engine below. All it would lead to was embarrassment, because he was probably only teasing her. Men had shown her time and time again that she wasn't worth it.

But Jessie cared, and Ashlynn felt safe with her, and that was where she planned to stay until her friend found someone. She wasn't naïve enough to think that their intimate relationship would last forever. It just allowed them to scratch an itch they both had, an itch that was now creating a completely different image in her head—one of her and Wesley naked.

As Ash's mind spun in circles, Wesley's thumb brushed her heated skin again, sending a shockwave between her legs.

"Stop doing that," she hissed.

"What?" he asked, his eyes wide and all innocent-like, as the corners of his lips twitched.

"You know *what*."

"Shut up," a man demanded from behind them.

Wes looked back at him. "Sorry about my girl, dude."

Ashlynn tried to pull her hand away. "I'm not your girl."

"Geez, will you two be quiet? You're like an old married couple," Justin complained. "I'm trying to listen."

"Fine," Ashlynn grumbled, wishing like heck she could wipe the smirk off Wesley's face. But instead she had to settle for sitting back and watching the movie, trying to ignore his fingers doing spicy things against her skin and Jessie's look of approval across the way.

Oh, Lord, kill me now!

Chapter Two

"I was kind of hoping we'd see them explode," Justin said as they walked back to the car after the movie. "It's like the writer spent the whole time building up their power, and we didn't even get to see a true glimpse of it."

"I hate movies where all the main characters die," Jessie whined.

Ashlynn pulled open the back door, waving her friend inside first. "At least they died saving the world."

"Ya, but they died saving it from themselves," Jessie said as she climbed inside. "Could you imagine never being able to be with your siblings because you'd bring about the apocalypse? They were literally each other's kryptonite."

Once they were all inside the car, Wesley pulled out of the parking lot and onto the somewhat empty road. The movie had ended at midnight, and most of the people in their sleepy little town were stretched out in their beds.

"Does anyone want to stop for a drink?" Wes asked.

"No, thank you. Jessie has to get to the set early, and I'm going with her," Ashlynn said.

Wes grinned as his gaze traveled down Ashlynn's body and back up again. "You guys are young. You can handle not getting enough sleep."

She shook her head, as did Jessie.

"If I show up with red eyes to my first main role, do you realize how many people will think I'm a drug addict?" Jessie said. "We better just get home."

"Do they still want you there at five thirty?" Ashlynn asked.

Jessie nodded. "If I knew it was going to be so early, I would have chosen a different job."

"It's the lifestyle of the rich and famous," Ashlynn quipped, rolling her eyes and grinning. If she'd had the courage, she would have loved to become an actress, but it wasn't her thing. Heck, she couldn't even lie if her life depended on it, so acting was out of the picture.

About twenty minutes later, they eventually turned onto the home stretch, a few blocks from her friends' place. Jessie had turned in her seat and was resting her head on Ashlynn's shoulder. The poor girl was drained, and who could blame her? She had been out practicing her lines with the cast all day. Ashlynn hadn't realized how much work actually went into learning their lines and their respective characters. She could never do it, but she did enjoy watching what went into a show's production, especially because Jessie was in her glory.

"Ash, did you want a ride ho—"

The sound of screeching tires drowned out Wesley's voice, and headlights lit up the interior of the car. Ash screamed as a vehicle rammed into their back passenger door on the driver's side, and the sound of metal meeting metal filled the air.

"Oh god," she cried as they were tossed into the air, the car's wheels leaving the road.

As the vehicle flew, it launched Jessie across Ashlynn's lap, and all she saw was her friend thrown against the window, shattering the glass. Searing pain ripped through Ashlynn's body as it got tangled with Jessie's. Her heart galloped as the world spun around her.

There was no flash of her life before her eyes, like some spoke of, as they rolled over and over down the hill. It was like everything in her head stood still, and nothing existed but the salt-and-pepper-shaker ride. She tried to brace herself but couldn't move. Her arms wouldn't listen. Fear hit her like a freight train, hard and fast.

They were all going to die.

In the last flip, her head hit the ceiling as it caved in, and her world went dark.

***

Ashlynn gasped, and her eyes flew open.

I can't breathe.

She reached up and felt tubes coming out of her mouth. She tried to yank them out, but her fingers weren't working as easily as before. She couldn't grip the tubes. A hand came to rest on her arm.

"Easy, hun. It's okay," a tender voice said.

The sound reverberated in her head like a gunshot. She tried to ease the mounting pressure by pressing her hand against her forehead, but she ended up hitting herself with something hard instead. Why didn't her hand feel right? Why was it heavier than she remembered? And why the hell didn't she know where she was? Panic bubbled inside her as images and thoughts flooded her mind. They were moving so fast that she couldn't grab on to a single one. She blinked her eyes and gave them a rub, trying to slow the images down, but when she did that, the walls in the room began to roll like waves on the ocean and her stomach followed suit. She closed her eyes and waited for the feeling to pass before opening them again.

"Is that better? I gave you something to help with the nausea."

She nodded gingerly, afraid that if she moved too abruptly, she'd become nauseous again.

"Do you remember what happened?" the same voice asked.

She turned her head towards the sound and vaguely made out a woman in blue scrubs. She racked her memory, trying to grab a thought out of the jumbled mess, but ended up shaking her head.

"Do you remember your name?"

The woman's voice sounded like a trumpet, making her squeeze her eyes closed with every word. She wanted to crawl back into the dark and stay there. Opening her mouth to speak, all she could do was croak because of the tubes.

Ashlynn.

Her name was Ashlynn. That she could remember.

"I'll go get the doctor and see if we can get those out."

Ashlynn reached for the woman, but her arm was heavy. Glancing down, she noticed a white cast reaching up to her elbow on one arm and a smaller one on the other.

"Don't worry. I'll be right back," the woman said reassuringly, giving her cast a little pat, which made Ash grunt in pain.

After the nurse left, Ashlynn tried to reach into the deep recesses of her mind and pull out a memory. But all she could come up with was the sound of tires screeching and the smell of chemicals assailing her nostrils. The rest was dark, like something was holding the memory hostage. None of it made sense. She felt like she was flying, spinning like you do on the Gravitron ride at a fair.

Attempting to sit up, she let out a cry when sharp pains engulfed her side and back, her neck burning. Her eyes filled with tears as she fell back against her pillow in defeat. And that was how she remained until the doctor and nurse came back into her room. They were sporting halos around their bodies but were less blurry than the first time she had opened her eyes. She just wished her head would clear a little too. It was a dark, foggy mess.

"Hello, Ashlynn, I'm Doctor Langston. I'm glad to see you awake. How do you feel?"

Unable to talk, she tried to raise her hand to do a thumb's down but failed miserably.

"Here, let's get the tubes out," he suggested, reaching for them.

Once freed, she asked, "What happened?"

"You were in a car accident," the doctor said before listening to her breathing with the stethoscope. "Airway sounds good."

"Accident?" she asked.

"Do you remember anything?"

"I have little snippets in my head, but they don't make sense."

"That's not surprising. You hit your head pretty good."

Ashlynn stared at the ceiling. The last thing she could remember was going to the movies with her friends. "Oh god," she cried, sitting up abruptly and screaming out in pain, her vision darkening, narrowing like a tunnel.

"Careful, dear. You are seriously injured," the nurse said, helping her to lie down again.

"My friends? What about my friends?" Jessie, Wes and Justin had been there too. The staff's faces turned downcast. "No. No. Just no,"

Ashlynn said, her stomach dropping into a bottomless pit, her chin wobbling.

"I'm here, squirt," Wesley said, limping into the room. Ashlynn looked around him, trying to find Jessie and Justin, but they weren't there. Wesley's face was swollen and covered in brown, blue and purple bruises. His hands were wrapped with gauze. He came over and wrapped his arms around her in a gentle hug. "Can you give us a moment?" he asked the staff.

"I just have a few more things to discuss before we go," the doctor said, his face going red. "Do you want us to talk alone?"

"Whatever you say can be said in front of him, too. I don't care," Ashlynn said. She needed someone with her that she knew, even if it was Wesley. The same boy that used to pull her pigtails when they were growing up, and the one she used to chase when he did. Even now, his fingers played with the ends of her hair flowing off her shoulder, like it was the most natural thing in the world.

"Okay," Dr. Langston said. "What pronouns do you use?"

"Oh god, you have to be kidding me." The tears that had been waiting to fall slid down her cheeks. She couldn't get away from the gender crap anywhere. "Why does everyone keep asking me that?"

"I'm sorry. It's just with the complications, we want to make sure that you are addressed according to your gender preference."

"My what? Will you tell me what the heck is going on?" Her insides burned with anger and rage. It was bad enough she had to be treated this way out in the world, but you'd think the hospital staff would be more professional.

"I'm sorry. I assumed you knew already," the doctor said.

"Knew what?"

"That you're intersex."

Ashlynn sat there blinking rapidly, ironic laughter bubbling in her gut, leaving her speechless.

Wes looked between the doctor and Ashlynn as he scratched his head. "What do you mean intersex?"

The doctor opened his mouth to talk, but then turned to her for confirmation before he did. She'd heard the term before, but had never bothered to look into it more deeply. Not even the schools spoke much about it, except for maybe teaching others to be more accepting of those who identified differently than their assigned gender.

Ashlynn glanced at Wesley and wondered what was going through his head. Maybe she should ask him to come back later after she'd finished speaking with the doctor. But before she could say anything, he gave her a reassuring smile and wrapped his large hand around hers, offering his support. There was no sign of laughter or disgust in his eyes. She gave him a shy smile before turning back to the elephant in the room.

"Has no one spoken to you about this before?" the doctor asked.

"No," she said, taking a deep breath. "What's this about?"

"When you were brought in, you were bleeding profusely, and we had to operate. That's when we discovered male and female reproductive organs."

"Male?" She repeated the word slowly, trying to wrap her mind around what the doctor was saying. "But that doesn't make any sense. Last I checked, I had a vagina."

"Inside your labia was a testicle."

Her jaw dropped. "A what? And what do you mean was?"

"We're not sure how, but it ruptured in the accident and we had to remove it."

Ashlynn stared at the doctor, dumbfounded. "But I have a vagina," she said, repeating herself. "I don't have a dick. I'm not a boy. I'm a girl, damn it!"

"Would you like me to bring in the hospital counselor?" the doctor asked. "They have experience with this type of thing."

Exhaustion overtook her and she let her head sink further back into her pillow, staring up at the ceiling, forgetting all about her hand being wrapped in Wesley's until he gave it a gentle squeeze.

"I think she's tired, doctor. Can you let her rest and then answer more of her questions later?" he asked.

She.

He.

It.

Oh god. She was an it. It was bad enough that she didn't look like an average female, but now even her insides were confused. She'd thought at least she had that going for her. Ashlynn pulled her hand away from Wesley's and rolled over with a painful cry. She buried her face in her pillow, trying to pull the sheets up to her forehead but failing miserably. Without even being asked, Wesley did it for her, and then brushed Ashlynn's hair from her face. She couldn't look at anyone right now.

"Can she have more pain meds yet?" Wes asked.

"Yes, I'll send someone in to give her some," Dr. Langston said before he turned and left the room.

"What do you want me to do, Ash?" Wes asked, gently touching her hip with his hand.

"Justin and Jessie?" she whispered. "Are they okay?"

He sighed sadly, his voice cracking. "Justin is a little worse for wear, but he'll be fine."

"Jessie?" she asked, her own voice hoarse as she rolled over to face him.

Wes's eyes filled with tears, his lips pressing into a grim, painful line. "She…she—they…"

He got up from the chair and sat down on the edge of her bed, appearing at a loss for words. Ashlynn couldn't ever recall seeing him cry before. He was always as cool as a cucumber—the typical macho man.

"It's not good, is it?" she asked, looking into his worn, tired blue eyes.

He tore his gaze away and stared at his black Nikes, his cheeks wet. His hands were in tight fists on his lap. "They say she's brain-dead. Mom and Dad are with her now. They're talking about pulling the plug, Ash."

Ashlynn sucked in her bottom lip as a black hole opened inside her, swallowing her stomach whole. "No. No," she cried, shaking her head. The room suddenly grew dark and all the light that Jessie had brought into her life escaped as her heart tore in two. Fighting to get up, she cried out in pain. "I have to go to her. I have to see her."

"There's nothing you can do, Ash," Wes said, guilt evident in his voice.

"You don't understand. I have to be with her."

"I understand more than you know, squirt," he said, squeezing her hand. "I know what she meant to you. But we were in a serious car accident, and you aren't in any condition to go anywhere yet."

"I'm fine. I can do this." Ashlynn tried to sit up and noticed the whiteboard at the end of her bed. "Why does it say it's the eighteenth?"

"You've been in a medically-induced coma for about a week."

A week? She'd been out for a week? "My mom and Carl?"

"They just went downstairs to get some food. They should be back soon."

"And do they know?"

"Know?"

"About my, uh, problem down there?" Ash asked, pointing to her pelvis.

Wes cleared his throat, his face turning red. "I… uh… I-I'm," he stammered. "I'm not sure."

"By the way, thanks for not running away."

Most men would have been repelled at the thought of holding hands with an alien like her. *Her.* That pronoun was now up for debate, wasn't it? How could she call herself a woman after having had that thing in her body? The word *it* felt more like the truth somehow. Wasn't that what you called something that wasn't one or the other?

An *it* or a *they?*

Ash pressed a cast-covered hand against her forehead, trying to ease the throbbing pain and stop the walls from moving. Her entire body felt like it was encased in lead and was slowly being dragged to the underworld. She closed her eyes, but bright flashes of light appeared with each throb, making her even more nauseous.

"I'll stay until your parents get back," Wes promised. "Just rest."

"Wes?" she said quietly, her voice barely even a whisper.

"Ya?"

"What am I?"

"You," he said, planting a gentle kiss on her forehead. "You're you."

His soft, warm lips made her skin tingle, and it spread like a summer breeze throughout her body, making her feel safe and secure. But his response didn't answer the question, and she was too tired to ask again, so she fell asleep wondering who she was.

***

When Wesley was certain she was out like a light, he let his finger caress her cheek. Her skin was baby soft. She moaned at his touch and the sound wrapped itself around his heart. There was something about her that called to him. Something different, surreal. She had a look in her eyes that took him to unchartered waters, drawing him in. He wanted to drown in them, but as soon as he caught her eye, she would look away, her cheeks turning red.

She felt something. He knew she did, but he had a feeling she was too scared to explore it. And he couldn't blame her, especially with all the bullying she had endured. It was enough to turn anyone off the opposite sex and leave them with self-esteem issues that would take a lifetime to fix. Ashlynn didn't deserve to go through that, and he was glad Jessie had taken the time to convince her she was worth it and beautiful.

Wesley thought the same. She didn't have the photoshopped figure that women had in magazines or the conventional movie star looks, but she had a heart that no one else's came close to, and a spark in her eyes that made him want to tease her, just so he could see it roar to life. She was more beautiful to him than anyone else he'd ever met in his life.

He desperately wanted more, but Jessie was the reason he'd held back from pursuing her. He knew they were in a relationship the day he caught them moaning together in the bedroom. When he took Ashlynn's hand at the theatre, he wasn't expecting Jessie to give them a look of approval, nor did he expect her to tell Ashlynn to go for it. Getting the green light had meant the world to him.

Now, here they were. God. How could so much have changed so quickly? He traced the scratch on Ashlynn's cheek and winced. It pained him to see both her and his sister lying in a hospital bed. Justin hadn't left his sister's side since it happened. He wouldn't even look at Wesley and blamed him for the entire thing. His parents had had to hold Justin back on more than one occasion.

So, Wesley had decided to come and sit with Ashlynn, giving her parents a much-needed break and him a chance to sort through his emotions. If he stared at his sister's broken body any longer, he would become a muddled mess, and his parents had it hard enough as it was.

It seemed so unfair that he'd walked away with a few scrapes and bruises and a sprained ankle, while everyone else had suffered so much more. He took a shaky breath, his chest tightening for the hundredth time that day. "Damn it," he muttered, as he wiped a tear away before it left tell-tale evidence on his cheek. If only he could go back in time and take a different route home. Then they'd all be sitting in their living room talking about the movie, instead of living in a nightmare.

But they were here, in this dang hospital. And one of them wouldn't be leaving. He lowered his head, resting it on the edge of her bed, unable to hold back his tears any longer. "It's not fair," he cried. It wasn't supposed to be this way. They should all be fine. Wesley clenched his fist, desiring very much to hit the person who'd done this to them.

A moment later, a hand came to rest on his head. He jerked upright with tear-stained cheeks, hoping it was Ashlynn, but it was just her mom, Claire. He quickly turned his eyes away, guilt assailing him.

"Sorry, I didn't mean to startle you," she said softly. "I didn't want to wake her up."

"Did the doctors touch base with you?" he asked.

"Yes. Thank you so much for sitting with her and for being here when she woke up."

He nodded and then quickly left the room before the tears in his eyes threatened to fall again in front of an audience.

Chapter Three

A few days later, Wes was staring at Ashlynn, who sat in a wheelchair across the bed from his sister, Jessie. His parents flanked him, resting their hands on his shoulder, showing that they didn't blame him. Yet they should. If he'd only paid attention and put his safe driving skills to use, they would never be in this place. They would never be in the position where…where…

Oh God.

He was the one who'd killed his sister. All he'd had to do was look left and right before entering the intersection. He shouldn't have cared that the light was green. He should have slowed down. Looked. Checked. Done something. *Damn it!*

They shouldn't be here. Ashlynn shouldn't be here. And it was beginning to look like Justin would have to give up his career because of the freaking accident. A deep ache filled Wes's soul. It was like a black shadow covering every corner of his being, sucking away any joy he had.

"It's time," the nurse said, walking up to the foot of the bed.

"Can't we wait just a little longer? She might wake up," his mother begged, her face wet with tears that wouldn't stop flowing.

"This was what she wanted, Jules," his dad said gruffly, pulling his wife tight against his side and dropping a kiss on the top of her grey-haired head. Jessie was an organ donor and had previously told them she didn't want machines keeping her alive. She had wanted the end of her life to mean something.

"But she's my baby. Please, just a little longer," his mother cried as she sat down beside Jessie, pressing her forehead against her daughter's. "Jessie? Sweetheart? Please… please come back to me." Sobs racked his mother's body as she clung to her daughter.

Wesley's chest tightened, and he struggled to catch his breath. His mother's pain hit him like a ricocheting bullet that broke into a thousand pieces on impact. He gripped the collar of his shirt, pulling it away from his neck. And, in a mad panic, his gaze darted around the room before falling on the one person he knew could help him.

Ashlynn.

He needed to focus on her.

And it would appear she needed to focus on him, too. Her eyes never strayed from his face. "I'm sorry," she whispered. He nodded, unable to speak, his throat clogged. This was really happening. It wasn't a dream or a movie. It was real life.

The police had declared it to be the other driver's fault, but he couldn't shake the feeling that there was something more he could have done. He knew Justin certainly thought so. He hadn't spoken to Wesley since that day, not like a brother normally would.

The accident played over and over in Wesley's mind. Maybe if he wouldn't have froze at such a crucial moment, he could have turned the wheel and the guy wouldn't have hit the back side of the car where his sister had been sitting. The screams. The cries. The twisting of metal. The flipping of the car and seeing his sister hit the window would forever be seared into his head. It was in his dreams and his thoughts whenever he closed his eyes.

The only peace he found was in the eyes of his sister's friend. She didn't look at him with hatred. She didn't shy away from him, didn't turn away. Ashlynn was the only one that helped him stay grounded, even though she had been lost in her own head too, confused by the intersex discovery. They hadn't really talked much about that, but he could see the confusion in her eyes.

Ashlynn reached over the bedrail and took her friend's limp hand, drawing Wesley's attention back to his sister. The nurse pulled the plugs from the wall, and the porter wheeled the bed out of the room, with them following behind. His mother stayed next to his sister's bed, holding her hand as they wheeled her down the Walk of Honor. Nurses, doctors, staff, family and friends lined the wall, flowers in hand. Ashlynn sang "There You'll Be" by Faith Hill as Wesley wheeled her down the hall right behind his sister's bed.

He sucked back a cry as her words struck him deep in his heart. His sister had been his light, pulling him back from the brink when he'd almost lost himself. His parents had completely missed his struggle and hadn't even noticed. But Jessie had.

Ashlynn reached up and placed her hand on his, giving it a compassionate squeeze. He brushed his thumb across her hand in response, drawing on her strength. Life wasn't fair. Jessie had been going places—more than any of them—and now she was gone.

The walk down the hall to the elevators was the longest walk he would ever take in his life. Once she went inside, they wouldn't see her alive again. They wouldn't even be there when she took her final breath. What if they were wrong? What if she could come back from this? What if the neurologist had misread the brain scan? He couldn't let them do this. Not yet.

"Stop!" he cried. Wesley rushed to his sister's side, framing her pale face with his hands. "I'm so sorry, Jessie. This is all my fault. Don't leave me, please."

The people around them clasped their hands against their chests, eyes full of unshed tears. And it made him want to punch something. What could they possibly feel? They weren't close to her. It was just another workday in the hospital for them. But for him, he would give anything to trade places with Jessie. If he had slowed down before entering the intersection, the car would have hit his door.

"It should have been me."

He buried his face in the crook of her neck as a fierce cry bubbled inside his chest, like the cry of a banshee. God! This couldn't be happening. "Wake up, damn it!"

"Son," his dad said, placing a hand on his back. "We have to let her go."

"No! We can't let them do this. We have to wait. We have to try," he begged, grabbing his dad's shirt with both hands. "She's not gone. She can't be." Wesley's shoulders shook as his dad pulled him into his arms. "I'll go. Let me go. Not her!"

Ashlynn rolled her wheelchair over to him and rested her soft hand on his. He collapsed at the foot of her chair, hiding his face in her lap, like a little boy. She nodded to the procession to continue amidst her own aching pain.

He turned his head and watched as they continued down the hall to the elevator. "Jessie," he croaked, his voice barely a whisper.

"I'm sorry," Ashlynn whispered, as she ran her hand through his hair, her tears landing on his head. He gripped her hand like it was his life raft, as though it could keep him grounded to this plane of existence.

As much as it hurt her to say goodbye, she knew it couldn't compare to what Wes felt, or even Justin. They were losing a part of themselves.

Jessie and the hospital staff entered the elevator, and it felt like time froze in the last millisecond before the doors closed. All she could see was her friend's smiling face in front of her and the joy that often filled the room whenever Jessie walked in. She was the light of their little family, a light that was snuffed out far too quickly. Suddenly, Ashlynn felt extremely tired. And sore, drained of every last bit of energy she had left.

"I-I need to lie down," she said, her eyes drooping.

That seemed to catch Wes's attention, and he got up, wiping his tears away with his sleeve. "I can take you back."

"No, that's okay. You need to be with your family. My mom can take me back." Ash nodded towards her mom, standing along the wall with her stepdad. She had a feeling that Wes and their family needed to be alone together. "Come see me later?"

Wesley squeezed her hand before walking over to his parents. They pulled him and Justin into a tight embrace. Justin stood stiffly, not hugging any of them back. He was frozen like a statue, and Ashlynn wished she could take their pain away.

Ashlynn's mom walked over and turned the wheelchair around. They made the trek back to her room, saying nothing along the way. There was nothing that could be said. The air was heavy with death and grief. It clung to her lungs like tar as she struggled to breathe. She needed to lie down. Her stomach was rolling and churning, and it needed a break from all the movement.

Once back in her room, her parents helped her into bed. Her mom helped cover her up, and Ashlynn hid under the covers, closing her eyes. If she saw the grief in her mom's eyes any longer, she'd burst out crying again, and her ribs couldn't handle it, neither could her pounding head.

"I'm just going to go to sleep. You guys can head home if you want," she said, knowing full well they both had work that needed to be done, and they'd already taken enough time off to be with her. They ran their own business, which needed them. "I'll be fine, really."

Her mom sat down on the bed next to her and brushed Ashlynn's hair away from her face. "You know this isn't your fault, right?"

"That doesn't make it any easier," she muttered.

"I know, hun. I'm sorry," her mom said, giving her shoulder a pat.

"I've got some good news though. The doctor said we might be able to take you home tomorrow."

Justin had been released the day before, and Wes hadn't stayed in the hospital as a patient, which was surprising. She would never understand how some people walked away without a single injury or something minor, while others paid for it with their lives. She was glad that Wes was okay, though. His emotional pain was bad enough as it was. He didn't need more physical pain on top of that. His eyes had lost their spark, the spark that was uniquely his. It could pull you in and wrap you in kisses before he even said a word.

"Hun, did you hear me?" her mom asked.

She opened her eyes and looked at her mom. Ashlynn hadn't even realized she was still talking. "Sorry, I zoned out. What were you saying?"

"The doctor mentioned counseling for you. I've found a few therapists not far from home."

"Counselling for what?"

"Well, the doctor figures with all the recent developments, you might need someone to talk to."

"Oh."

They had brought someone in from their on-site trauma counseling team, but they all seemed to want to talk about the discovery and not the accident. She wasn't ready to talk about either one yet. In fact, the last thing she wanted to talk about was her gender, or more accurately, the lack of one, or the nightmares that plagued her, which surprisingly weren't even about the accident. They were about being surrounded by people who treated her like a freakshow in a circus—laughing and pointing their fingers at her. In her dreams, the adults were worse than the kids.

The discovery was embarrassing, even more embarrassing than just looking different. Now there was a genuine reason for it, a cause. But it meant she wasn't who she thought she was, a real girl. Instead, she was the thing people joked about.

"I'm going to sleep, Mom. I'm tired."

She closed her eyes, and her thoughts drifted back to her friend. Jessie wouldn't have cared about the latest discovery. She had told Ashlynn, on more than one occasion, that she loved her just as she was. What was Ashlynn going to do without her? Who would she tell all her secrets to or visit when she needed to feel normal? Jessie would know exactly what to say, and it pained her to realize that she'd never hear her voice again.

Ashlynn squeezed her eyes closed and disappeared under the covers, hiding from her parents who, after a few minutes, kissed her on the head and then filed out of the room, leaving her alone.

"Oh, Jessie," she murmured.

Chapter Four

Intersex.

The word stared at Ashlynn, in huge monster lettering on the computer screen, getting bigger and bigger by the second, like it was haunting her. She didn't want to be intersex. All her life she'd been taught she was a girl. An oddly looking one, but a girl nonetheless. It was what she'd fought for. But she'd been lying to herself, and the bullies had had it right all along. Thanks to one rogue testicle, her body was now a stranger, and she didn't fit into any one gender. How was she supposed to live that way?

She'd known she had something in her labia, but her doctor had insisted it was a cyst. It hadn't hurt. It had just felt weird if she ever masturbated. Ashlynn gently flopped backward on her bed, spreading her arms wide, casts and all, letting out a sigh. It wasn't enough that her entire body hurt, her spirit had to get in on it too.

Wasn't she supposed to know who she was at nineteen years old? Especially her own gender. They were all taught about gender chromosomes in science class. If you had XY, you were a boy. XX and you were a girl.

Were her genes too stupid to figure that out? How could she be both, or neither for that matter? What kind of freak of nature was she? Ash ran her hands down her face and groaned. Would she ever know the answer to that question?

Her doctor had suggested contacting a peer support group to meet other people like her, but she wasn't ready to face anyone yet. Her stepdad didn't know what to say or even how to look at her. Her mom had just refused to address the issue since they'd left the hospital and was acting like it didn't exist. It made her glad not to have any siblings to deal with. They'd probably rib her as good as any other kid.

"Ash?" her mom said, stepping up to the doorway of Ashlynn's room. "We have to get going to the clinic."

She was getting her casts off today. Six weeks had passed since the accident, and she was ready to have full use of her arms again. "I'll be right down, Mom," Ashlynn said as she reached for her shoes under the bed.

But instead of finding her shoes, her fingers closed around a box, which she pulled out and placed on the bed. It was a box of memories—a type of scrapbook—that she and Jessie had started together when they were kids. After the funeral, Jessie's mom had given her a few things to add from her daughter's personal belongings, including the script Jessie had been given for the television show.

Shuffling through the items, Ashlynn picked up the dolphin ring Jessie had given her at their graduation. Jessie had a matching one and had been buried with it. Ashlynn slipped it on her finger as a tear blazed a path down her cheek. It was hard to believe that Jessie was gone and they wouldn't be able to go after their dreams together.

"Ashlynn, we have to go," her mom yelled again.

She put the lid back on the box, grabbed her shoes and stood up, then limped her way downstairs.

Once she was ready, they filed outside. Ashlynn stopped on the last step, staring at the car. Fear rushed through her like a tornado as wave after wave of anxiety swirled down her spine. Her chest tightened, and her breathing grew shallow.

Images of bright lights flashed before her eyes as the crunching of metal and the screeching of tires drowned out the sounds of her mother's voice. Ashlynn covered her eyes, trying to block out the memory. Her stomach rolled violently as she remembered her friend flying across her lap. Ashlynn sat down onto the bottom step, her head in her hands, eyes filling with tears.

Her mom sat down beside her. "What's wrong, hun?"

"I can't. I can't do it."

"We have to. We already postponed the visit once. Come on," her mom encouraged. "It's only a short drive."

Ashlynn looked at her mom's car. It was a tiny hatchback. Wes's car was bigger and higher, and it had still fared badly. It had been a total write-off. "Your car isn't safe. It isn't. I can't do it."

"I'll drive slowly and carefully."

"I'll take the bus," Ashlynn finally decided.

"You'll be late."

"I don't care. I'll be safe."

"I know you're scared, but I've been driving for twenty-five years and haven't been in a single accident yet," her mom said, touching her knee gently.

"Well, yippy for you!" Ashlynn snapped, pulling her leg away. She didn't need to hear about her mom's good luck, not while hers was steadily going downhill. First, it was her looks, then the accident, and now her insides. She was a bad luck magnet.

Her mother let out a breath. "I don't know what to say, except you'll be fine."

"You don't know that."

"Please, get in the car."

"I already told you I'm going to take the bus."

"Don't be ridiculous. It's just a short, simple car ride."

"You don't get it, do you? I just about died in a simple bloody car ride, Mom."

"Don't use that tone with me. You can't be late for your appointment or they might not be able to see you. And we need to know if everything is healing okay."

"Then stop arguing with me and let me catch the bus. One comes in five minutes."

Ashlynn grabbed onto the railing and pulled herself up to standing. There was absolutely no way she was going to get in that car, or any car for that matter. The ride home from the hospital and the one to the clinic two weeks ago had been enough for her.

"I think we need to talk to the doctor about your anxiety."

"Why?" she asked. "So he can send me to the loony bin?"

Ashlynn turned away from the sadness and frustration that was evident in her mom's eyes. She couldn't understand. No one could. And the one person who'd ever understood her was gone. "Oh Jessie," she murmured as she limped back into the house.

"I'm ordering you to get in the car," her mom demanded.

"You can't order me around like I'm some little kid."

"I think waiting on you hand and foot for the last few weeks has earned me that right," her mother said, her voice rising. "Now, get in."

Ashlynn refused to listen to her and grabbed her bus pass from inside the desk near the door. Couldn't her mother understand that she was as frustrated with all this as she was? Did she think Ashlynn wanted to be afraid of driving or even stepping outside her own front door? It was all so frigging overwhelming that she couldn't help it.

Without even shutting the door, Ashlynn rushed by her mom. She figured her mother would have grabbed her if there was a spot on her body that didn't hurt. Ashlynn heard her sigh and the door slam as her mom disappeared into the house.

Ash walked about half a block to the bus stop and waited there, watching the cars go by. With each roar of a motor, her chest tightened, and she struggled to breathe. She felt like, at any second, a car would hop the curb and come directly towards her. Stepping behind the little bus alcove, she put the glass wall and bench between her and oncoming traffic.

A lady who had her grey hair wrapped in a bun and wore a long thick skirt turned to look at her. "Are you okay? You look pale."

"I'm okay, thanks," she said, giving her a weak smile. She wasn't going to air her grievances when there were a couple of teenage boys standing off to the side. They were already looking at her like she was crazy.

"You look like you've been through a lot," she said, nodding towards Ash's cast. "You can sit with me if you'd like."

"Thank you," she said again, ignoring the boys snickering. "But I'm fine."

The lady smiled sympathetically and turned to face the road again. Ashlynn knew the woman didn't believe her for a second, but she was grateful for the silence and reprieve. Even the boys had turned their attention to a video they were watching on one of their phones.

Soon, the bus pulled up to the stop and Ash limped her way to the door before taking a step to get inside. It was crowded, and there was only one seat all the way in the back, between two boys. She hesitated before making her way towards them, groaning. The trip was twenty minutes, and there was no way she'd handle standing the whole time, holding onto something. She'd fall over, and with her luck, break another bone, or elbow some poor gentleman in the face.

Ashlynn sat down and watched as the two young teen boys edged away from her, like she was going to give them cooties. Did she really look that bad? Maybe she should just resign herself to the fact that she was a human pariah. Or was she even human? There were two genders, male and female, and she didn't seem to fit in either category. It wasn't like she was a mutant with cool superpowers. That would be something she could live with.

But to know everyone was right about her burned her heart into a tiny little crisp, and the one person she could count on to help her feel normal was gone. She had no one to talk to. No one she cared to talk to. The darkness gathered strength inside her soul, eating away at any peace she had left, like piranhas feeding on their prey.

If this was what life was all about and the way it would go, she wanted no part in it. She was done. Finished. This world was not a place she wanted to be. Anything had to be better than this.

Ten minutes later, Ash pulled the yellow cord to get off at the next stop. Forget the doctor. She didn't need anyone's help anymore. All she needed was to close her eyes and never wake up.

Chapter Five

"Hello?" Justin answered, holding the phone up to his ear while Wesley looked on.

They were just getting ready to settle into watching *Rush Hour*. It was Wesley's last night home before heading back to work at his summer job near the university he attended. He had been off since the accident but was well enough to return now. Justin was still off, but doing much better. He wouldn't be able to return to his warehouse job, but he was considering going to college. All Justin had to do was figure out what he wanted to do with the rest of his life.

Wes still felt bad that he hadn't been able to avoid the accident and that he'd chosen a vehicle with a poor center of gravity. If they wouldn't have flipped, then the accident may not have been as bad as it was. But he had to face the fact that it had, and they'd lost Jessie. The one person who'd had huge ambitions. Huge dreams.

He also hated that Ashlynn had lost her best friend. She hadn't been the same since the day they left the hospital. Everything had been going as well as could be expected, until she'd started refusing their calls. They'd tried to stop by her house, but her mom couldn't get Ashlynn to open her bedroom door. She'd withdrawn from everyone and everything. Things were going downhill fast.

Growing up, she was the sweetest thing he'd ever met—always going out of her way to be friendly to people, even when they weren't always the friendliest to her. There was something special about her. Something real. And you don't find that very often.

Turning his attention back to the phone call, he heard Justin say, "No, sorry. We haven't seen Ashlynn."

That had to be her mom on the other end of the line. Wes looked at his watch. It was eleven at night. Why wasn't she home yet? She rarely ever left the house anymore according to her mom.

"I'm sure she's fine." Justin paused for a moment, apparently listening to what Claire was saying. "She missed her appointment too? That's not like her at all." He paused again before responding. "Sure. If we hear from her, we'll let you know."

Wesley had already slipped his sweats on over his shorts and his shoes before his brother hung up the phone. Justin wasn't in the position to spend the night looking around for her, but he could. His ankle was feeling much better. "Where's her favorite place?"

"There's a spot in the bushes near her place, but I'm certain she wouldn't go there at nighttime," Justin said.

"Anywhere else?"

Wesley had a bad feeling. He'd seen the pain in her eyes the last time they were together. It was deeper than he'd ever seen it before. And quite frankly it scared him.

"She likes the view from the train trestles, and the lookout point on the outskirts of town."

Those were three leads. Hopefully, one of them would pan out. He wasn't going to let anything happen to her if he could help it. They had already lost Jessie. He had no plans on losing Ashlynn too.

"You don't think she would hurt herself, do you?" Justin asked.

"I don't know to be honest."

"Out of all of us, she was the one that could find the light in any situation."

"This might be the one time that she can't."

"She couldn't have it any more difficult than we do."

Wes held his tongue. Ashlynn hadn't spoken to Justin about the intersex deal, and it wasn't up to him to broach the topic, but he sure as heck could make sure she was safe and didn't hurt herself, even if he had to bring her back here and not let her out of his sight.

"Keep trying to call her and text me if you hear anything. I'm going to get going." Grabbing his jacket and his car keys, Wesley rushed out of the house and into his new SUV with all the safety features you could get. His new car would keep him and others with him safe.

He pulled his seatbelt across his body and secured it before driving to the first location, the lookout point. He hoped to God he had picked the right one, because if he was too late, he'd be up shit creek without a paddle. Ashlynn wasn't the type of person to just disappear, not unless there was a problem. And she had them in spades.

Turning onto a narrow gravel road, he slowed down, having taken this drive numerous times before. It was the most dangerous drive in their town. There was a steep drop on one side of the road, leading all the way back down. Straight down to be exact. No concrete barrier stood between him and certain death. His gut told him she wasn't up there because there was no bus service to the top, but it still had to be checked. She could have hitchhiked.

He finally drove around the last corner to where the lookout started. It was a wide grass field that spanned the width of the hill. Picnic tables lined the edge, which was blocked off by a fence to prevent anyone from accidentally falling off. Wesley grabbed his flashlight and shone it around the area. No one was there except one lone car parked off to the side. He didn't recognize it, but, even so, his heart thumped as he walked up to it. Wes knocked on the window.

When it rolled down, a big, football-player-sized man was glaring at him, his brows drawn together in frustration. "What do you want?" the guy snapped.

Wesley leaned down to look inside and noticed a girl with her shirt half unbuttoned and her skirt hiked up to her waist. He breathed a sigh of relief. It wasn't Ash. "Sorry. I'm looking for a girl."

"Well, you can't have mine, so piss off."

Wesley pulled out his phone and selected Ashlynn's picture to show him. "I'm looking for her. Have you seen her?"

"No, but you can keep her if she looks like that."

Without thinking, Wes tightened his fist and planted it on the guy's chin with a sharp left hook. "Never talk out of your ass like that again." He stepped back before the urge to hit the guy attacked him again.

The man went to step out of the car, but the girl grabbed his arm, shaking her head. "Let him go."

Wes shone the flashlight around one final time before returning to his car, annoyed with humanity. Ash had the heart of an angel and the eyes to match. He wasn't going to let anyone diss her or put her down, nor was he going to let anything happen to her.

His next stop would be the train trestles. It was the middle point between their place and hers. And he knew the two girls had always walked across the bridge to go to the small swimming hole on the other side. It was a popular hangout for teenagers, especially those who wanted to drink without their parents' approval.

Wesley pulled his car off to the side of the road near the entrance and stepped out, shivering when a breeze tickled the hairs on the back of his neck. Grabbing his jacket, he slammed the door and locked his car. It was a good five-minute hike down the trail to the bridge. The train trestles ran over the one and only gulley in their town, which had a creek full of big rocks at the bottom. The water wasn't too deep this year. They hadn't seen a lot of rain over the summer.

He pushed his way through the overgrown bushes until he reached the start of the tracks. This portion of the railway hadn't been used in years, so he didn't have to worry about any trains passing through. The track led to an abandoned warehouse where kids often went to party, aside from the swimming hole.

The area was quiet tonight and it made him thankful to have his big Maglite. Otherwise, he wouldn't dare go clomping through the bush like this, not when cougars were known to grace this area of town. A branch snapped behind him and he spun around, shining the light at the noise, his blood pumping. The light crossed paths with red eyes, but he let out a breath of relief when a rabbit emerged instead of a predator.

"Don't do that," he grumbled at the animal.

Taking a breath, he continued towards the bridge. He wasn't sure what he was going to find or whether he'd be prepared for the discovery. His mind was going in all sorts of horrible directions, including seeing Ashlynn's brain smashed on the rocks below and the creek turning red with blood. It was too easy to see it, and he couldn't get the image out of his head.

So when he turned the final corner and saw her standing there on the edge, all thought stopped. He raced to where she was and pulled her back from the edge, falling backward on the bridge, with her on top.

"What the hell?" she screeched as she struggled to get away, but he refused to let her go. He was never going to let her go again.

"Stop, Ash. It's me," he said, giving her a squeeze.

"Wes?" She turned in his arms to look at him, accidentally elbowing him in the crotch in the process. "Oops."

He groaned, losing his voice momentarily as red-hot pain coursed through him.

"Sorry about that," she said, scrunching up her cute little nose. "But what are you doing here?"

"Looking for you."

"Is Justin with you?"

"Nope, it's just me. But now it's my turn to ask a question," he said, sitting up and ensuring he still had a secure hold on her arm, grateful that he'd found her. "What are you doing here?"

Ashlynn glanced back to where she'd been standing moments ago, having been unable to find the courage to jump. It was only the fear of the unknown that had held her back. But she couldn't seem to go home either, because her fear of the world was just as prominent.

"You weren't… you know…" Wes asked, letting his voice trail off.

"No, I—" She stopped talking when he raised an eyebrow at her, as if saying he wasn't stupid. Ash sighed and tried to pull away from him, but he had a vice grip on her arm. "Please let me go."

"Not until I know you aren't going to do anything stupid."

"What's it to you?" she snapped. "It's my body. I can do what I want."

"I know, and you're right, but I care about you, Ash."

The tone in his voice made her ache for what she knew she could never have. No man would want her, especially knowing she could never give him kids. She'd never be a real woman. There was no place in the world for someone like her. She'd always be the outcast.

"Talk to me," he begged softly. "What's bothering you?"

"I don't want to spend my entire life defending myself from the world or fighting with myself over who I am," she said as tears filled her eyes and an ache rose inside her. "And I don't want to live without the one person who saw me for me."

Wes gathered Ashlynn into his arms, pressing her cheek into his chest. "I see you, Ash." And when the clump grew in her throat, not allowing her to speak, he spoke again. "I see you."

"Ya, as your little sister's friend. But you don't know me, or what I am either. I'm not normal."

"So what?" he said, refusing to let her go when she tried to move away. "Normal is highly overrated."

"That's because you're normal."

"Who defines normal? In my eyes, Ash, you are the most incredible person I've ever met. You may not fall under the world's definition of male or female, but things are being redefined all the time. The decision of who we are going to be is as much our choice as what we're going to do with our lives. That doesn't fall to anyone else to decide but you. And only you."

"Do you really think so?" Ash asked hopefully.

"Very much so. It's what I like most about this generation. We have more freedom to be who we are, and to choose what we are, than any other generation before us."

"And who do you want to be, Wes?"

"A man who is given a chance to be with you."

"Me? But what about—"

"I don't care about that," he interrupted.

Could it be true? Could he actually care about a person like her? Her mind doubted his words, but her heart wanted to grab on to him and never let go. "But what will others say if they find out?" she asked, her green eyes glistening.

"Have I ever cared about what others think?" he asked, brushing her tears away.

Now that she thought about it, he did pave his own way in life. He never cared what anyone thought about his career path as a fashion designer, like how it was too girlie. He still chose to go after it, regardless of the rumors spread about him. So maybe he was telling the truth. Maybe he really did like her, as she did him. She hadn't realized exactly how much she cared about him until he'd walked onto the bridge like a guardian angel.

"Are you really choosing me?" she asked.

"Yes," he answered. "Now, it's my turn to ask you. Will you choose me too?"

"Why does this feel like we're on a Valentine's Day game show?"

"Roses are red. Violets are blue. I've spent my life searching for one such as you."

She pushed against his chest, laughing. "You're so cheesy."

"You know it." Wes grinned. "So, what say you, Ashlynn Jacobs? Do you have room in your heart for me?"

Ash looked into the eyes of the first man to choose her, woman or not, and saw no malice in his gaze, just gentleness and admiration. As she pondered his question, a weird feeling sparked to life in her chest, and she found herself saying, "Yes, but I'm not saying I love you yet."

He stood up and held out his hand. "I'll settle for you agreeing to come home with me tonight."

"That works for me." And this time, she took his hand willingly.

The End

The Holy Trinity
Viola Russell

Thursday, April 4, 1968

"You'll be late for your guitar lesson." Trinity heard her mother's voice and glanced in the direction of the kitchen.

"Today is volleyball practice, Mom. Not guitar." Trinity looked at her mother and then turned her attention to the letter Siobhan had sent her. She'd settled onto the couch in the living room of the large shotgun house and read every word with longing. Trinity looked in the direction of the kitchen. Pots and pans rattled as her mother prepared dinner.

Grace Fischer was everything her daughter was not. Leggy but curvy with blond hair cascading around her shoulders, Grace exuded conventional femininity and Southern elegance. The floral sundress hugged Grace's hips becomingly as she moved from the kitchen to the hallway and then the living room. Trinity sighed. She would never look like her mother. She was too bony, angular, and flat-chested. Her build made her a great soccer player, but she was not anyone's definition of a conventional beauty. Hair just stringy and brown, tall but not a model's figure.

Trinity slipped the letter under her leg as Grace approached. She'd received another short letter from Siobhan, but her mother couldn't see it. Grace wouldn't approve of her friendship with Siobhan, but the messages slipped to her in the hallway of Alexander Hamilton High School made Trinity's day. Ever since she'd met Siobhan at Palmer Park when she took the dog for a walk, Trinity had felt stirrings for the other girl she couldn't quite understand. That was last summer, and Trinity had enjoyed walking her dog as Siobhan slowed her jogging to keep up with her. Then, Trinity found herself in the same high school as Siobhan, one that catered to the academic elite.

"Well, get your gear. You don't want to be late." Grace glanced absently at Trinity before heading back to the kitchen.

Trinity headed down the hallway of the old New Orleans shotgun that she shared with her parents, slipping the note into her jeans pocket as she did so. Siobhan provided some meaning to her life. Her family had moved to New Orleans from Texas five years before when her father resigned his commission as a chaplain in the United States Army and took a position as pastor of a church in New Orleans. The move itself was not unusual for Trinity. As a military brat, her family had moved often, but she'd had trouble assimilating here. The culture was unlike any she'd ever experienced. The city was a mixture of ardent Catholicism mixed with voodoo. Old Southern manners mingled with a certain decadence. Trinity had stared with fascination when her parents had ventured into the French Quarter and seen street performers. Young men and women sauntered around in clothing so flamboyant they could have been costumes.

Even the Carrollton neighborhood where she lived perplexed her. Many of the locals knew each other for years; most of the kids her age had gone to local schools, local Catholic schools at that, for most of their lives. Cliques abounded.

The family had left Texas during her junior year. Trinity was used to the rootlessness of military life, but this move had been devastating. She'd met Sarah and had experienced the first physical stirrings she'd ever experienced. When she'd started high school in Austin, her parents had encouraged her to date "nice" boys. Her father produced a parade of pimply adolescent males before her, the sons of military officers he'd come to know. Trinity had dated one briefly; Jake had been a nice, nondescript young guy with brown hair and a stutter. Trinity saw him as no more than a friend. Then, she met Sarah. She was confident and popular—the kind of girl that attracted boys and won the friendship of girls. When Sarah smiled at Trinity, Trinity's heart pounded and her palms moistened. Sarah's presence made it hard for Trinity to breathe.

Of course, she could tell no one this. Her father was an old-fashioned minister and a true Texan. Reverend Nathan Fischer would have considered his daughter's thoughts deviant and immoral. Not that her mother was any more liberal or accepting in her thinking. Grace's father also had been a minister. She believed that a woman's duty was to marry and have a family. She tolerated Trinity's love of volleyball but found her daughter lacking in feminine charm or Southern grace. Well, Trinity knew she had little grace.

Trinity had reveled in her role as one of Sarah's entourage. For months, a group of fellow students accompanied them to movies, shopping trips, and parks. Trinity wasn't sure that Sarah returned her affection in the same way until they were alone one day at Sarah's house, studying for a biology exam.

"Would you like iced tea?" Sarah looked up from her textbook. They were sitting beside each other in the dining room, notebooks and textbooks stacked between them.

"Yeah, sure," Trinity replied absently and continued scribbling in a workbook. Girls like Sarah didn't want girls like her. They married handsome Texas cattle ranchers and had babies. She risked a glance in the direction of the kitchen.

Sarah returned with the iced tea and placed one glass beside Trinity. She suddenly leaned forward and placed a lingering kiss on Trinity's lips. At that moment, Trinity's world changed. Her nipples grew pert; her insides resonated with an all-consuming heat. Nothing had happened after that, nothing physical. Trinity suspected that Sarah kept other company with some of their school friends, but she still longed for that sweet kiss again. Then, her father left the military and found a church in New Orleans.

Trinity suspected Nathan Fischer had resigned when he read the fine print about a tour of duty in Vietnam. Until then, her father's postings had been easy, educational for Trinity and her brother Liberty, and exciting for her parents. They had toured Europe while they lived on the base in Germany, had traveled the United States, and had accumulated relationships along the way. In spite of his boastful patriotism, Trinity suspected her father had no desire to see real battle.

Settling in one place was hard on Trinity. Not, however, on her brother. Liberty had settled into his new school and life with ease. Well, he was like that—blond and handsome with an easy smile. He graduated high school with honors and made his way to Tulane on a scholarship.

Settling into a new place hadn't been so easy for Trinity; then, she'd met Siobhan that fateful day in the park.

"Hurry up, honey. You'll be late for your practice." Grace's voice broke Trinity's reverie. She pushed into shorts and tennis shoes, snatched the ball from the corner of her room, and strode out of the door, switching off the light as she did so.

Trinity wasn't that into volleyball, but Siobhan was. Trinity would do much to have Siobhan's company. When they pulled into the school parking lot, Trinity saw that her father was already there. He'd expressed more enthusiasm than her mother at the prospect of her playing volleyball. Trinity winced when she remembered his words. "Grace, we should let her do it. She's not involved in anything. She's not like Liberty."

Not like Liberty. No, definitely not.

"Did you have a snack before the game?" Nathan slipped an arm around her and kissed her forehead. He walked beside her and Grace as they made their way to the gym.

"Yeah, I know about keeping my blood sugar up." Trinity glanced at her father and grinned. Nathan inspired devotion—in his daughter and his congregation. When she was a child, he'd read to her at night and had encouraged her childish writing.

"Hey, Trinity! We're about to start warm-ups!" Siobhan approached, her red hair falling in waves around her shoulders. She flashed a warm smile Trinity's way and snatched the volleyball. She added quickly, "Hi, Mr. and Mrs. Fischer."

"Hello, Siobhan." Grace managed a smile. Trinity sensed her mother's disapproval of her friend. She knew her mother would see Siobhan as too confident, too bold, not well-mannered in any conventional Southern way.

Nathan, however, smiled broadly. Trinity saw her father's gaze take in Siobhan's shapely legs and pert breasts with approval. "You girls have a good game." He patted Trinity on the shoulder.

Trinity jogged toward the gym with Siobhan. The building was an old one, built in the early 1900s. Peeling paint adorned the outside of the building. The bleachers squealed as young people pounded upon them, and the students had adorned the wall with posters boasting the superiority of various classes. A senior poster flaunted the upcoming graduation. The mingling of dark and light shades of blue had been Siobhan's idea. Siobhan had created the interlocking images that looked Celtic or rune-like. Teachers had raised their eyebrows, but the principal, a free thinker, had smiled indulgently.

"Will you come to my mother's house after the game?" Siobhan bounced the ball as they walked.

"I'll ask my parents after the game." Trinity held open the door. A warm liquid filled her midsection with Siobhan's invitation. She liked Siobhan's mother. She was beautiful like Siobhan and wore flowing dresses and flowers in her hair. She was probably as old as Trinity's parents, but she seemed younger.

Trinity held the door open for her parents. She heard their conversation as they entered. Her father was talking. "I'd like to watch the news tonight. That agitator King is talking somewhere. You know I believe in Christian charity toward people, but you can't just condemn your government. In theory, I believe in equality, but I don't think the world is ready for that kind of equality. It has to be gradual."

Her mother looked around her and then said in a hurried whisper. "Well, so do I, but people all have a place in this society. Disrupting the natural order isn't wise."

Trinity ventured a glance at her friend. She noted a grimace on Siobhan's face. Siobhan's expression indicated amusement, even disgust. Trinity's cheeks burned. She couldn't meet the other girl's gaze. Siobhan obviously saw Grace and Nathan as unsophisticated rubes at best and bigoted Neanderthals at worst. Trinity, too, didn't understand her parents' hypocrisy. Her father preached Christian charity, but Trinity had heard him pontificate in the same bigoted way before. He espoused equality for minorities "in theory." In theory. Trinity laughed at the hypocrisy.

She remembered making her way to her father's office one night when she couldn't sleep. She'd retrieved a text by Luther from a bookshelf and began reading. Nathan had underlined numerous derogatory comments on Jewish people. Trinity hadn't remembered any of her Sunday school teachers discussing Luther's more controversial stances. In fact, the Bible stories she'd remembered were full of God's chosen being eaten by whales or warning others of God's vengeance.

The game was hard fought. The muscular, working-class girls from the regular high school easily defeated Trinity's geeky team. After the game, Nathan patted Trinity's arm affectionately when she jogged over to their place in the bleachers.

"It was a good game, honey. You got some good hits in."

Trinity released her hair from the ponytail. "Dad, please don't lie." She looked at Siobhan who was gathering her gear by the bleachers. She looked from her mother to her father. "Can I eat dinner at Siobhan's house?"

Grace grimaced and then tried to smile. "Well, sweetheart, I—I don't know. I was hoping we would have a family meal tonight. Liberty isn't bringing his girlfriend over. It would be just us." She turned to Nathan. "Nathan, what do you think?" Was it Trinity's imagination or did her mother sound desperate, afraid?

Nathan slipped an arm around Grace. His gaze took in Siobhan and her mother, talking at the other end of the gym. "I think it will be all right, Grace." He looked at Trinity. "Remember how we brought you up, your values. If there's something you don't feel comfortable with, you call us."

"Sure, Dad." Trinity nodded and turned in the same direction. For the first time, she saw Siobhan and her mother as her parents did and understood their anxiety. Siobhan stood beside her mother in her volleyball uniform, her shapely legs attracting the interest of several boys who passed her way. Ripe nipples pushed against the blouse she wore. Trinity wore the same uniform but didn't look as sensual or as daring. Maybe it was the mane of dark, red hair that flowed just below Siobhan's shoulders or the way her laugh reverberated throughout the gym when other students approached her. Trinity instinctively understood that Roisin, Siobhan's mother, elicited her parents' true trepidation. She owned an art gallery on Magazine Street, the mecca for arty shops and boutique clothing. Siobhan had mentioned that her mother read tarot cards on the weekend and belonged to some religion called Wicca. Trinity wasn't sure she understood just why the mother and daughter were so threatening to her parents, but she also saw that there was much she didn't know—even though she hadn't been totally sheltered as a military child.

"Yeah, sure. I mean, we're just going to study for a history test for tomorrow." Trinity turned on her heel just in time to see a boy approach Siobhan and place a lingering kiss on her lips. A hard desire to rush the boy, a classmate, and punch him possessed Trinity, but she simply bit her lip. Siobhan only laughed and slipped an arm around his neck.

Patty, the volleyball coach, approached the pair in horror. With long gray hair, Patty looked like a witch from some fairy tale. The girls joked that her skin was a tad green. "This isn't your parents' couch, Kevin. Ask her out for a real date if you want that."

Roisin only laughed. "Oh, Patty, get a life. We may be old ladies, but these kids have a life to live."

After an early vegetarian dinner, Trinity and Siobhan sat together at the table with their history textbooks and notebooks spread out before them. Trinity had never eaten an only vegetarian meal, but Roisin had said that meat polluted the body and the mind. The home was minus a television. Roisin said there was no need to cloud the mind with unnecessary clutter. However a radio played very sensual blues in the background. Roisin was in the kitchen. Trinity could hear her body swaying to the music as she gathered the dishes.

The house wasn't unlike Trinity's own home, but it seemed much more open, inviting. Her mother's kitchen was too dark. This house was filled with light. The kitchen was a magnificent white; paintings lined the walls, and exotic vases and art adorned the furniture.

Suddenly, the music cut off. The voice of the DJ broke a brief silence. "This is insane! A sad day! Reverend Martin Luther King has been shot in Memphis! What a blow to the Civil Rights Movement." The DJ went on to expound on King's accomplishments and how tragic his loss was.

Roisin's dancing and singing had come to an abrupt halt. Trinity swallowed and stared at her friend. Siobhan's eyes were wide and too dark, shocked. Roisin stood in the doorway, tears glistening in her blue eyes. She moved to the girls and placed a hand on Siobhan's shoulder. Siobhan turned to her mother, hugging her at the waist. Her shoulders shook as she wept, her face buried in her mother's dress. "Why do they always kill people who want peace and unity?"

"They always do, darling. They kill the prophets. They killed Jesus, didn't they?" Roisin stroked Siobhan's hair.

Trinity didn't even realize that she, too, was weeping until she placed a hand on her face and felt a tear blotting her cheek. She placed a hand on Siobhan's back, and Roisin covered it with her own. Trinity would always remember this image of the mother and daughter. Their bond was unbreakable.

Later, Trinity and Siobhan sat together on a picnic bench in the backyard. Siobhan sighed. Trinity followed her gaze. A large crow approached a small sparrow as it settled on the birdfeeder. The larger bird spread its wings; the tiny bird took flight but not before collecting seed in its beak. The small transistor radio perched on the bench hummed "All You Need is Love."

Trinity broke the silence. "So you and your mother followed King?"

Siobhan lowered the volume on the radio. "Definitely. We drove to

Washington to hear him speak."

"So your mother doesn't think he's a rabble-rouser?" Trinity thought of her own parents and their professed Christianity.

"No, of course not. He preached peace and reconciliation." Siobhan looked at her, apparently incredulous. She added softly, "It's so sad, but like my mother says, they kill all the prophets, even Jesus."

Trinity felt the blood rush to her face. Did she sound like a real rube to Siobhan, who was so sophisticated? When they'd moved to New Orleans, Trinity had felt that she was much more worldly than her counterparts. New Orleans was one big small town. Many of the people had lived in the larger metropolitan area their whole lives; ties of family, school and church connected them. Consequently, many had little experience of life outside their city or state. As a military dependent, Trinity had experienced more of the world, but she'd never met anyone like Siobhan.

Siobhan placed a hand on hers. "King was right. The Beatles are right. We need love in this life." She wiped away a tear. "Why can't we just have love and not judge? Why do people want to hurt each other?"

Trinity shook her head. Siobhan's hand felt warm, soft, and comforting. She wanted to encircle her friend in a warm hug. It was then that Siobhan leaned against her and pressed her lips to Trinity's. Her soft, wet tongue pushed into Trinity's mouth, and a warm, liquid sensation filled Trinity's whole being before settling within the depths of her stomach and pulsing through her most intimate parts.

Trinity had very little romantic experience. Her parents were always very protective of her and vetted any boy who had the temerity to come calling. When they didn't return for any second date, Trinity wondered if she was just unattractive or if her parents hadn't scared them away with their intrusive questioning.

But this kiss was like nothing she'd experienced and filled her with warmth and a burning heat from her head to her feet. She pushed away first, confused by her own desire. Her hand instinctively went to her mouth.

"I'm sorry, Trinity. I thought you felt the same." Siobhan smiled kindly, her hand still over Trinity's. "I like you a lot."

"It—it's just that I saw you with Kevin." Trinity remembered the envy she'd felt for their male classmate when he'd kissed Siobhan and Siobhan had returned his kiss.

"Kevin is beautiful. I love beauty. Life is too short not to have beauty." Siobhan gazed at her questioningly. "We don't have to go further if you don't want to."

Trinity had no answer. She was confused, even a little frightened by the feelings overwhelming her. "It—it's late. I'd better go." She wanted to hold Siobhan and then run away. She'd savored the other girl's wetness in her mouth. What would her parents say had they seen this intimate moment?

"Do you need a ride home?" Roisin looked up from her dishes as Trinity entered. "I can drive you. It's getting dark."

"No, no thank you. I'll be okay." Trinity needed the walk, the air. She collected her books from the table and made her way home.

When she passed Siobhan's next-door neighbor, she saw the curtains rustle and remembered that the house belonged to Mrs. Mary Schmidt, a church member. She raised a hand to wave, but if the woman was behind the curtain, she made no response.

Trinity placed her key in the lock and listened to the familiar click. She pushed open the door. The car was there, but the house was too still. Where were her parents? Liberty's old Chevy was parked on the street as well. Only as she closed the door did she hear muffled voices in the kitchen. Was her mother weeping? She heard her father's voice, a desperate hiss.

It was then that Liberty appeared in the hallway. He was as stunning as any Greek god, even in shadow. His blond hair fell softly around his shoulders, and the T-shirt he wore hugged his toned form.

"What in hell did you do, Trinity?" He moved to her, took her arm, and propelled her toward the door. "Mom's saying you're dead, and Dad's talking about sending you away." He paused, stared at her, and whispered. "I heard words like deviant, perverted. It was about you. They called your friend's house, looking for you."

"Oh, shit!" The words escaped Trinity's lips. "I wonder if Mrs. Schmidt saw—"

"Saw what?" Liberty opened the door and almost pushed Trinity onto the closed-in porch. His gaze bore into her.

"No—nothing." Trinity turned away and walked to one side of the porch.

"You can tell me." Liberty stood behind her and placed his hands on her shoulders. "I take care of my little sister."

Grace emerged from the kitchen, tears blotting her cheeks. Her dark eye makeup was running. "How could you do this to us?"

Trinity stared at her mother, shocked. Siobhan lived two streets over. How could her parents know? Then, she remembered Mrs. Schmidt. "Mom, I—I don't know what you're talking about." The words flew from her mouth before she could stop the denial. Of course, she knew what they meant. Old Lady Schmidt had called them.

"Hasn't enough happened today?" Nathan moved within inches of her. Liberty stepped closer to her. "That subversive King dies, and all his bleeding-heart followers are mourning and whining. Then, you prove yourself a deviant."

"Dad, relax." Liberty glared at his father. Trinity saw his fists clench and unclench at his sides, and she suddenly realized that Liberty felt as she did. Her parents were hypocrites and liars. "You have one woman's rumormongering mouth as confirmation of anything about Trinity. Why are you listening to someone else?"

"We don't hear her denying it." Grace strode over to Trinity and bellowed into her face. "Do you deny kissing that filthy tramp? Do you deny any of this?"

Shame and confusion overwhelmed Trinity. She saw how she looked in her parents' eyes—as something foul and wicked. She blinked away burning tears as anger replaced the shame. Trinity suddenly realized she couldn't change who she was. She had no "choice" in the matter, and her parents were judging her, judging who she was. Christians! She guessed they had conveniently forgotten the pronouncement, "Judge not lest you be judged."

She almost spat the answer. "Yes, I kissed Siobhan. I enjoyed it."

Grace gasped and recoiled from Trinity as if she were a snake, her mouth a gaping chasm. "How—how could you admit to such filth?"

"We didn't bring you up to engage in such behavior." Nathan placed protective, almost restraining hands on Grace. "This is a Christian household, and I cannot have my family behaving in an ungodly manner."

A massive hole opened in Trinity's heart. Liberty stood by her side and looked down. He placed a protective hand on her shoulder. Trinity looked from one parent to another.

Her father spoke. "You will never see that—that girl again. You will go to a Lutheran school in another state and remember who you are." He paused and took a breath. He looked at his wife. Grace was nodding vigorously. "Some of these schools specialize in turning young people like you. Placing them on the right path, the godly path."

Trinity's words were a scream, a massive echo in her own ears. "I have never been ungodly! I loved going to church, to Sunday school! I even didn't mind teaching the little kids in Sunday school."

"Something you can never do again." Nathan's face darkened. "No one, not even my daughter, can corrupt little children."

Loss overwhelmed Trinity. She crumpled into Liberty's arms. "I—I can't live without Siobhan, and I won't go away to some school where they think I'm crazy or the devil." I can't live without Siobhan. It was the first time she'd let herself even think—let alone say—just how she felt about Siobhan.

Breaking away from Liberty, Trinity threw open the door and stumbled onto the porch. Liberty followed at her heels, calling her name.

"Trinity! Trinity! Where are you going?"

Trinity turned back and fell into her brother's arms. Her mother called from the door. "Come back here! You're not going anywhere without our permission!"

Nathan's voice soon joined in the chorus. "Trinity! You will come here this instant! You are going to do what your mother and I say!"

Trinity looked up at Liberty. "I can't go back in there."

"Where do you want to go? Don't worry." Liberty placed a hand under her chin, raising her face to his. "You can stay with me. Angela won't mind."

Trinity sniffled and nodded. Angela was his girlfriend. They lived in a stately old uptown house in the university area that had been converted into apartments. Their parents didn't like Angela any more than they would like Siobhan. She was too beautiful and Italian. Their father had warned Liberty about such girls.

"Does she live with you?"

"Yeah, Mom and Dad wouldn't like that, either." Liberty grinned and slipped an arm around her shoulders.

Trinity managed a smile. "It will be crowded with me there."

"We have room. You're my sister. I won't let you live on the streets." Liberty drew her close, and Trinity wept against him. His protective kindness was overwhelming.

Later that night, settled into a small room in Liberty's apartment, Trinity called Siobhan and told her what had happened with her parents.

Siobhan's voice on the other end soothed Trinity and also made her heart beat hard. "I'm sorry to hear about that. The old bitch next door always wants to cause trouble for us. I'm sorry you were dragged into it."

"They won't take me back, not without me giving you up and going to some weirdo place." Trinity's voice caught on a hard sob. Deep within, she felt as if her world was crashing around her. A gaping hole of hurt seeped through her body. What if she'd been wrong about Siobhan? What if she'd misinterpreted the other girl's feelings? Trinity had seen her friend kiss their male classmate with equal passion. She swallowed and said the words. "I think I love you, but I don't know if you feel the same. I never loved anyone like this, so I don't really know. You kissed Kevin and liked it."

Siobhan laughed, that easy and silvery laugh. "I like pretty things, pretty people. Kevin is pretty. For me, it's not about men or women. It's about pretty people."

Trinity took it in. Her parents had taught her that sexual love was sacred. Such easy thinking mystified and troubled her. "I don't want to lose everything."

"Your parents may come around." Siobhan was the counselor, the sage, the advisor. "You can count on me. You're more special than Kevin."

Trinity suddenly felt lonely, small. "I'm not pretty."

"Yes, you are. Stop thinking about yourself like that." Siobhan sighed, obviously exasperated. "Hey, come over tomorrow. We can study together. My mother is working late. She has to do some inventory in her shop." She added softly, "I think you're pretty, and you need to feel that way, too. Pretty is a state of mind."

The next day, Trinity watched Siobhan at school. She envied her friend's easy confidence as she chatted with friends and other classmates. Trinity had never been so at ease with other people. Siobhan flirted with everyone—females as well as males. Her easy smile won over teachers, counselors, and administrators. At best, Trinity fit in with the woodwork. At worst, she was the awkward, unsociable girl. Maybe she could learn from Siobhan.

After school, Trinity made her way to Siobhan's house. She avoided passing her parents' home, imagining them still stewing over her departure and what they could consider her brother's heresy. However, she passed by the church on her way. Standing in the shadow of an oak tree, she saw her parents arriving for the weekly choir practice. Nathan shook the choir director's hand before stepping over the threshold of the church. Her mother laughed and smiled with Jerry Georges, the choirmaster, before stepping through the heavy wooden doors and into the church. Trinity darted into the street and made her way to Siobhan. She was grateful to Liberty for taking her in, but his bliss with his girlfriend Angela only added to Trinity's emptiness.

"Hey, come on in. My mom made tea this morning. We have some brownies, too. Mom gets them from Lawrence's bakery." Siobhan led Trinity into the den, turned, and suddenly clasped Trinity to her. Trinity dropped her textbook and fell into the depths of her friend's warmth. Siobhan's lips were sweet against hers. Burning desire for Siobhan filled Trinity as Siobhan pressed her tongue gently against Trinity's lips, prying them open. A burning liquid burst inside Trinity, traveling from her midsection to her most private parts.

When Siobhan released her, she took her hand and said, "Come with me." She led Trinity down the hall to her bedroom.

"I—I've never been with anyone." Trinity felt panic sweep over her. "What if—"

"Don't worry. It's simple. It doesn't matter if it's with a guy or a girl." Siobhan smiled at her—the sage, the leader.

Trinity followed Siobhan to the bed. Siobhan ran a hand over her breasts as she let her lips linger over Trinity's lips and then travel to her neck. Trinity felt her body respond to Siobhan's caresses. A simmering heat traveled through her spine as Siobhan's hands found her most intimate parts, stimulating her throbbing need. Then, Trinity was actively responding, engaging with her partner. She threw off her blouse and helped Siobhan push out of hers, sucking on the other girl's breasts and then kissing Siobhan's toned midsection. Siobhan ran a caressing hand over Trinity's breasts as they came together in a passionate kiss, and then, suddenly, she was at Trinity's legs, kissing her thighs until the burning liquid flowed through Trinity to her throbbing sex. Siobhan's lips nibbled at her thighs and then moved to Trinity's soft stomach. Trinity quivered with awakening passion as the other girl's wet tongue caressed Trinity's pubis until her tongue traveled to Trinity's gateway to paradise. Waves of pleasure like an electric shock vibrated through Trinity. Her cries of pleasure echoed through the room as ecstasy filled her.

Later, Trinity lay in her lover's arms. "I never thought anything could be that good."

"It doesn't have to end." Siobhan reached into the table beside her bed, extracted a bag of cannabis, and began rolling a joint.

"What do you mean?" Trinity didn't want this to end, not ever.

"Well, we'll both go to college soon. We won't always be at the same school." Siobhan lit the toke and glanced at Trinity with that easy smile.

"Right. I guess." Trinity hadn't considered the broader future. Without her parents' support, she didn't even know if college was in her future.

"Next year, we'll have to apply to college." Siobhan inhaled the joint and passed it to Trinity. "I'm thinking of California, Berkeley. I could study art, teach."

Trinity hesitated but took the joint. With shaking hands, she put it to her lips.

Siobhan laughed. "It's not a snake. It doesn't bite."

"I just never have—" Trinity took a puff. The hot smoke filled her lungs, and she coughed. The after-sensation wasn't unpleasant.

"It's okay. It just gives you a buzz." Siobhan took the joint and inhaled again. She continued, "Anyway, you should come, too. Don't you want to major in history?"

"Remember, I don't have parents helping me anymore. I have to get a job after school to help Liberty since I'm living there." Trinity thought about Berkeley. The family had lived in California once. She'd loved it.

"Trinity, I'm sorry if I got you in any hot water. I didn't want that to happen." Siobhan turned to her.

"It's not your fault. It's my parents and their hypocrisy." Trinity caressed her friend's face. No, Siobhan was right. Trinity needed a new start, but how would she get that with her newly depleted resources?

A week later, Liberty picked her up from school in his old Chevy. He'd worked on the car, painted it dark blue, and adorned it with shiny new tires. She'd just slid into the passenger seat when he'd said to her. "I have news. The folks want to see you."

"Why?" Trinity's heart beat like an anvil. Even though her parents had been unfair, she still loved them. They were her parents and had supported her throughout her whole life so far.

Liberty shrugged. "I don't know. Dad called last night after you went to sleep and said they needed to talk to you."

Together, she and her brother headed to their father's home. The house seemed to be in darkness as they approached. However, a lone light shone in the kitchen. They made their way to the kitchen door and knocked. Grace opened the door and stepped aside to let them pass. Her mother's eyes were red-rimmed. A stray hair had escaped from her French braid. She awkwardly pushed it away. Grace never looked disheveled. "Your father and I want to talk to you."

Nathan emerged from the hallway. He looked older and drawn. "Trinity, as your mother said, we want to talk to you." He moved to his wife and slipped an arm around her shoulders. He indicated the sofa. "Let's sit down."

Trinity and Liberty sat on the sofa across from their parents. Trinity glanced at her brother and then at her hands in her lap. She swallowed hard. Her heart beat fast when she found her voice. "I—I can't change who I am. I never asked to feel a certain way for a girl—or a boy for that matter."

Nathan twisted the wedding ring on his finger. He looked at his wife. She nudged him gingerly. "We—I shouldn't have judged you so harshly."

Grace slipped her hand into his. "It was wrong of us, honey." Her voice caught. "The house isn't the same without you. You don't have to live with Liberty. We know it's crowded with you and his girlfriend there." Grace turned quickly to Liberty. "Oh, and you definitely can bring that young lady over for Sunday dinner. We welcome her to the table."

Nathan cleared his throat and ran a hand through his hair. "We also don't want you to miss out on college. We know how important that is. Maybe we can discuss it after dinner on Sunday." He added hastily. "Of course, Trinity, your—er—friend is also welcome."

Trinity's heart melted. They were both trying so hard. She crossed over to her parents and embraced them. He held her tight. "What if I want to go out of state? California?" She added softly. "Siobhan's going to California for college."

Nathan shared a glance with his wife and then kissed her forehead. "What can we say? I'm a failed minister. Too much of my life has been feeling superior and judging others. Sure, if you want California, we'll support it."

Liberty coughed. "Dad, you didn't fail us. Trinity and I both loved the church. We loved Sunday school. You didn't fail us."

"I failed somewhere." He drew Grace to him. "Someone we both respected—our choirmaster at church—took his life because his family couldn't accept him. He was a talented man. I'd known his parents. I must have not shown my congregation about true charity if they could so reject their son that he would commit suicide."

Trinity suddenly felt sick. Handsome Jerry Georges! She knew him. How could his seemingly gentle and loving parents reject him? She stammered, "I—I'm so sorry to hear that."

Grace stifled a sob as she said, "We don't want to lose you like that, my darling."

A genuine smile graced Trinity's lips. Her heart soared as her parents embraced her and Liberty.

December, 2020

"I'm so glad to see you ladies now open since the pandemic." The young woman with sandy blonde hair advanced to the register with two books clasped in her hand. Her brown eyes twinkled, and she smiled through her mask.

"Well, this bookstore has been our dream since we left Berkeley and came back to New Orleans. No Covid-19 is going to keep us down." Trinity smiled brightly, took the books from the woman, and began entering the prices into the cash register.

"Well, my daughter loves your children's books, and it's so nice to meet a real author here and know that you own this shop." The woman gathered the bag of books Trinity handed her.

"Yes, I love writing. I studied it in college, and my partner still provides all the artwork. She's the visual artist, just like her late mother." Trinity adjusted her Grateful Dead mask.

As if on cue, Siobhan took her place beside Trinity. She'd been in the office, completing work on the artwork for their next joint literary venture. She smiled. "Look for the new book next year."

She smiled at Trinity through a mask that blared, "Peace and Love."
"You can't keep us down. We follow our dreams."

The End

Midnight Queen
Annabel Allan

I strummed the guitar softly, humming along to the tune that had been stuck in my mind all day. I shook my head, trying to get my platinum blonde bangs out of my blue eyes. I decided I liked what I had, picked up my pen and wrote down the lyrics.

My cell phone went off. A little bloop sound that told me it was Snapchat. I looked at it, seeing her name, not really thinking much of it. She sent me funny pictures every so often, but in reality we hadn't seen each other since high school, more than ten years now.

I put down the pen and my guitar. I then grabbed my glass of white wine and the phone, sitting back on the couch lazily.

I opened up the message as I took a sip of the wine. She had Nickelback blaring in the background, a song I recognized. She stuck out her pierced tongue provocatively, then tipped back a pint of beer. She then did a little sexy dance to the beat before she pulled her top down, revealing her naked breast, her nipple a little bud.

I spit out my wine, closed the app and placed my phone on the couch, nearly throwing it away from me. I coughed a little, and some of the wine stuck in my throat. I wiped my chin, my eyes going wide as I looked at the phone. To say I was surprised was an understatement—it was mainly because of who was sending it.

Since I had her on social media, I knew she had come out as bisexual the year before, and I was bisexual too. It was something everyone knew, as I was very open sexually, and about my sexuality. For some reason, that made the band even more popular—girl band, girl crushes.

I wasn't surprised because she had sent me the sexy video, but because I thought she had a boyfriend. I thought she even lived with said boyfriend. I really thought I would be the last person she'd send a sexy message to.

I put down the wine glass and quickly grabbed my phone. I opened up Facebook and typed in her name. Her profile came up, and I clicked on it. I scrolled down a little, seeing that her relationship status was suddenly "single". I stared off for a moment, trying to process it.

I would be the first to admit that I'd had a crush on her in high school. Long strawberry blonde hair to her tiny waist, a nice hefty chest, her bright green eyes. She was actually classically beautiful, but she had an edge that I could never put my finger on. All the guys wanted her, that was for sure.

I was the weird artsy kid, and everyone assumed I was into girls. It was a uniformed Catholic school, and everyone made that assumption because they were jerks. If you're weird, you're gay, right? I decided to push against it, declaring vehemently that I was not.

Did it stop the feelings? She was my girl crush. My first girl crush, something you don't really forget. She was even my friend, my best friend at one point. I always thought maybe she was into me, but again, I was the weird kid. Artsy, into heavy metal, and honestly, just weird.

Cue my sexual awakening. Then I realized it was totally up to me who I liked or loved, and as much as I was attracted to men, I was also attracted to women. I didn't care who had opinions on it either. I embraced it and even dated the same sex a few times. I was single though, had been for nearly three years, and apparently, now so was she…

I still was unsure of what to do, but I didn't want to leave it too long, since the app told her that I had looked at the video. I opened up Snapchat again and decided to play it cool.

>That was provocative lol

I waited, my heart beating quickly. Was it a mistake? Was it meant for her boyfriend? Was she drunk?

She typed back, my phone vibrating.

>You love it.

"So, definitely not a mistake," I said, blinking several times. Then I typed:

>I did. It was pretty hot, just unexpected. What does your bf think?

I stared at the screen, seeing she was typing.

>What bf? Old news, babe.

My eyes widened again, looking about the room. I brushed back some hair, tucking it behind my ear, the ends tickling at my jawline. I had to play this very carefully, as I didn't want to come off as, well, weird.

>It was very sexy, not gonna lie.

She quickly typed back.

>I'm kinda slutty that way lol

I smiled a little to myself.

>I really don't mind...

Her reply came:

>I wouldn't mind if you sat on my face.

My eyes widened again, as I felt that little shock of sexual desire. I could feel my nipples hardening at the thought of it. There was no denying that the closeted sixteen-year-old Catholic school girl in me was squealing in delight.

I didn't want to keep her hanging, but I wanted the perfect response. I got up from the sofa, pacing back and forth until I decided I was going to be bold. I pulled up my grey sports bra and snapped a picture of my own chest. I then took a deep breath and clicked send.

She replied.

>I would love to stick my face in those.

I could feel my thighs thumping, the sound of my heart in my ears, the blood rushing through me heatedly. I could only think about the fact that she had moved to my area. Would a late night sexcapade be out of the question?

I was still confused. So, of course, I had to be me and try to dampen the mood with my inane questions.

>Where is this coming from? You do know I had a crush on you in high school, right?

She typed back:

>If I had known, I would have fucked you then.

I felt a little dizzy, trying to focus on how to reply to that. But she sent another message, catching my attention.

>What are you doing rn?

I licked my lips, feeling a nervous flutter in my stomach.

>Nothing really...why?

A few seconds went by, then all of a sudden she replied.

>I'm all alone...

Again, I was trying to think of a perfect reply. I also had to weigh my options at this point. She was probably a little drunk, horny, and knew I was bi. I was a logical choice to message for a quickie. I had also abstained from sex for three years, trying to focus on my music career.

I had gone three fucking years. I was horny as fuck, especially for her.

>Address?

I sent the message.

It took her a minute to reply with the address of her place, adding a little winkie face.

She knew.

***

When I looked up her address, I realized I lived thirteen minutes away from her. And those were the slowest thirteen minutes I have ever experienced in my life.

My car was a beaten-up little VW Beetle; it ran great but was considered an antique at this point, as I was still driving it back in high school. Even then it wasn't brand new, but I'd taken good care of it.

I gripped that steering wheel hard as I swerved through the midnight streets, my panties soaked at the thought of Lita Holliday. There. I'd said her name. Lita Holliday. My girl crush from high school.

I had changed into the only lingerie I owned—a sexy black lace bra complete with matching G-string. I also put on whatever was in reach, which happened to be a baggy band T-shirt—Ronnie James Dio's Holy Diver—and cut-off jean shorts. I slipped on my Chuck Taylor Converse and my studded leather jacket and got on my way. I really didn't want to make her wait any longer than I had to.

I stopped in front of her townhouse, parking on the street. I looked into the rear-view mirror, making sure my shoulder-length bob was sleek and straight. I hadn't put makeup on. In fact, I had been prepared to go to bed and had even washed my face clean of my day.

My hand shook as I smoothed down my bangs once again. I was beyond nervous about breaking through the friend barrier. Once Lita and I had sex, that was gonna be it.

I gave myself a little pep talk, nodding my head. I then got out of the car, putting my keys in the pocket of my jacket. I had a little clutch, with my ID in it as well as my cell phone, the band of it wrapped around my wrist.

I walked up the path, looking around. It was definitely a nice part of the neighborhood. I stopped at the door and took a deep breath before I rang the doorbell.

It took her twenty seconds to get to the door. She opened it, a smile on her pretty face. Her strawberry blonde locks were up in a messy bun, her sparkling green eyes on me excitedly. I noticed she hadn't changed from her video. She was still wearing a white tube top and blue pajama pants.

"Hey you," she said.

"Hey," I replied nervously.

"Come on in," she said, backing up so I could come inside.

I stepped over the threshold, trying my best to not act nervous. I was, though. I was definitely nervous, my thighs feeling like Jell-O as my stomach did a little flip.

She looked the same as in high school, just as beautiful, her skin immaculately clear, though she now had her nose pierced. She still looked like a Roman goddess, a little curvier than when we were sixteen, but in the sexiest way. She was still tiny, shorter than me, with a nice dip at her waist.

She closed the door behind me before walking past me. She led me into the living room. Her pint glass was on the coffee table, filled to the top.

"You can take off your jacket," she said, pointing to the couch. "Want a drink?"

"What do you got?" I asked, as I did as she said, taking off the jacket and putting it down on the arm of the sofa.

"Beer. Wine. Think I have some coolers," she said.

"Uh, wine sounds good. White if you have it," I said, sitting down.

"You got it," she said. She turned, sticking her tongue out a little flirtatiously as she went into the kitchen.

My hands were still shaky as she brought back a stemless wine glass and handed it to me.

"Thanks," I said, trying to steady my hand.

"No problem, babe," she said, sitting down next to me.

I looked around the living room, from her big TV above the fireplace to her directly. "Nice place."

"Thanks," she said, keeping her eyes on me hungrily.

I smiled a little, putting the glass down on the coffee table in front of me. I summoned my courage. "I was surprised by your video. Even more so that you invited me over."

"Why is that?" she asked, tilting her head to the side.

She shifted towards me, closing the distance. I felt my heart speed up, since she smelled amazing. Not girlish like in high school, but more…

well, womanly. I looked into her eyes as she brushed my hair away from my face gently, her face getting close to my own.

I felt my breathing start to get uneven, the desire in me making my face tint with a blush. "I don't know, I just—" I started, licking my lips. "I never thought that Lita Holliday would want to fuck me."

"I have for a while," she said, her hand moving to my thigh, stroking it lightly. "Why wouldn't I?"

"I guess I just didn't think that you were ever interested," I said in a breathy voice.

She put her lips up to mine, almost pressing them to me. "As I said, I would have let you ride my face then too."

I felt a shiver of delight run through me, my nipples hardening, my breasts themselves aching. Our lips were already almost touching, so I went for it—I pressed mine against hers, timidly at first, until she opened her mouth, inviting me in.

I slipped my tongue inside, holding her face gently to deepen the kiss. I don't know why I had ever thought that it would be sweet with Lita; it was definitely hot and passionate, our tongues entwining, slipping from dancing in her mouth to mine, then back. I had those butterflies in my stomach, flapping around as my mind couldn't get over the fact that I was full-on making out with her.

Her hand went from my thigh up to my breast, taking hold of it and squeezing. I gasped as I pulled away for a second, but she was quick to pull me back in. She only let me pull away once again when she took off my T-shirt, tossing it down on the floor.

She leaned forward, kissing my cleavage, as the bra I had on was a push-up, so there was an ample amount. She moaned a little as she squeezed both my breasts, licking and kissing my skin. Her hands went around to the back, and she unclasped my bra and pulled it off, leaving me naked from the waist up.

She didn't waste any time, diving for my left nipple and taking it into her mouth. She sucked on it, her tongue ring feeling especially amazing, driving me crazy. I let out a moan as my sex gushed out wetness, my clit almost painfully engorged.

She paid expert attention to one breast before moving the other, looking up into my eyes as she took my right nipple into her mouth. She bit down gently before sucking on it, flicking her tongue. My back arched, as I didn't want her mouth off of me.

She then kissed down my stomach as she got down on her knees before me, her fingers working at the button and zip on my shorts. I lifted my hips as she pulled them off, and her hands went to my G-string and took that off as well. I was, at that moment, glad I had shaved the day before, though I took to only shaving the lips of my sex and leaving the top trimmed.

She didn't seem to mind as she pushed my legs wide open, stroking my thighs. She kissed just below my belly button before she moved to the crease of my thigh, licking and kissing it attentively.

I could feel the wetness dripping out of me, and I lifted my hips once again in anticipation that she was going to dive in and eat me out. However, she moved over my sex and kissed the opposite side, licking that crease of my thigh. It drove me nuts. I panted heavily as my sex clenched, empty, but wanting.

She kissed above my sex, trailed down to my mound, then licked up my cleft. My stomach twitched deliciously, and I pushed my hips up one more time. She smiled a little, spreading the lips of my sex and giving a little lick to my clit, making me pulse. I let out a whimper, wanting more.

She flicked my clit with her tongue several times before she dove in and sucked on it. My body convulsed and shook, feeling the orgasm on the tips of my fingers, the pleasure rocking through me. She didn't let up, caressing up my stomach to my breasts, which she took in her hands, squeezing as she ate me ravenously.

It was building so fast that I felt a little light-headed. I then felt a deep pulse within me. Then another, and another. Until finally the pulses sped up, running together and exploding, my body jerking forward as I came. I held her head as I bucked into her face, coming so hard that I let out the loudest moan of my life.

She didn't let up, letting me ride out that orgasm until it was just little sparks here and there. She then pulled away, licking up my cleft once more, making a yummy sound, not wasting a drop.

She kissed my stomach, making me laugh a little, as it tickled. She then moved up to my lips, kissing me again. The passion intensified once more. I guided her down on the couch, laying her back. I pulled down her tube top and grabbed hold of her breasts, which were easily a double D. They were big, but not in an unpleasant way—they were actually quite fucking perfect, the right one pierced.

I kissed her once more before I moved to her left breast, taking her nipple into my mouth, tasting her. She moaned, biting at her bottom lip, which was probably the sexiest thing I had ever seen. I sucked on her nipple hard, making her chest thrust up as she whimpered. I then kissed down her stomach, past her belly button piercing, grabbing those pajama pants and pulling them off.

I felt my sex clench, as she wasn't wearing any panties and was shaved completely. I could see her wetness glistening on her lips, enticing me.

I caressed her bare thighs, spreading them wide, as she had done to me. I then kissed her inner thigh, trailing them up, skipping over her sex and trailing them back down the opposite thigh. I could smell her, the musky desire, which drove me crazy. I had to taste her.

I spread her lips a little, licking them clean first. I then flicked at her clit, making her moan loudly as she grabbed her breasts and squeezed them. I caressed my tongue up her cleft to her little clit and sucked it into my mouth.

She pushed her hips up, thrusting her sex into my face. I could sense she was getting close and pulled away from her, which made her sigh frustratedly. I smiled a little, drawing my index finger down her lips to her entrance. I paused for a moment before I pushed my finger inside of her depths, which clenched onto me.

She licked her lips. "Mmm."

I pulled my finger out and licked my index and middle fingers, tasting her again. I then pushed both fingers inside of her, making her whimper as she squirmed beneath me. She was tight and warm, velvety to the touch.

I slipped my finger out and back in again several times before I twisted my fingers, my palm up. I then leaned down back into her sex, found her clit with my tongue and sucked as my fingers slipped in and out. "Oh my God," she called, grabbing my head and raking her fingers through my hair.

I sped up my fingers, fucking her with them fast. I could feel her G-spot swell, knowing she was getting close once again. Only, this time I didn't let up; I sucked her clit as I fingered her, her walls clenching down on me until she erupted into tremors, coming hard. She nearly screamed from it, her grip on my hair tightening. I felt wetness gush out over my hand and into my mouth, and I lapped it up.

Once her body cooled, I licked her clean. I then kissed her stomach, up to her breasts, biting at the side of them. She giggled a little, pushing me with her shoulder before she kissed me once again.

I was so sure that after we'd both got off, that would be the end of it. But as her tongue twisted around mine, I could feel myself getting hot with desire once again. Who was I kidding? This was only the beginning.

***

I had slipped out close to six in the morning.

Lita was still sleeping and I'd left her a text saying I'd had a great time, but I had work later on in the afternoon. Though I was a musician, I wasn't a full-time musician just yet. I worked as a bartender and sometimes waitress at a local bar, which was good for paying the bills.

I hadn't received a reply all day, though I'd slept most of it. The night of hot sex had left me exhausted, but I will admit I'd dreamed of Lita and more hot sex. I didn't know if it was going to be a one-time thing or if we were going to make it a regular itch we scratched. There was definitely a sexual pull to her, but I was unsure if there was the emotional basis to establish a relationship.

These were the thoughts that filled my mind, putting me on autopilot while I was working behind the bar, filling drink orders. I had my back to the bar as I filled up a glass. I turned to place it down to see none other than my ex-boyfriend. I felt my heart jump into my throat and nearly dropped the drink.

I hadn't seen Gunner James for three years. I hadn't even heard about him in the band circuit. He was the lead guitarist of a fellow metal band. His brunette locks were just as luscious and long as I remembered, his black bandana with a skull on it holding them out of his face, revealing those baby brown eyes. He was the typical heavy metal kid, and boy, did I wish I could walk away from him.

"What are you doing here?" I asked, placing the drink down on the bar quickly.

"Nice to see you too, Cher," he said.

"Gunner," I said, shaking my head. "It's been three years."

"And I'm back in town," he said.

I crossed my arms. "So?"

"I wanted to talk," he said.

"I'm working."

"I didn't mean right now," he said. "Can we talk after your shift?"

I leaned on my palms against the bar. "What is there to talk about?"

"If you let me see you after your shift, you'll find out," he said, giving a little pout of his lips.

I stared at him for a moment, taking a deep breath. "Fine. Meet me at the loft, I'm off at two."

"Great," he said with a little smile.

We stared at each other for a while, the heat between us obvious. It hadn't been lack of passion that had broken us up. We were always passionate about each other. We always wanted each other. I still wanted him, in fact. I was just too tired to get into the same old fights, at least at that second.

He nodded a little before he stood from the stool, walking away from the bar without another word. I kind of knew that he felt it… but again, I didn't want to deal with it. I shook my head, trying to clear my mind of those thoughts.

I went to turn when I felt my phone vibrate. It was a text message— from Lita. My heart pounded inside of me and my stomach flipped. I opened the message, smiling a little as I read it.

>Free tonight?

I wanted to instantly reply hell yeah, but then I remembered that I had plans. I looked up, watching after Gunner as he left before I looked back to my phone.

"Shiiiiiit," I said to myself.

Everything in me wanted to see Lita again. Honestly, I had a sense she didn't want anything serious, which was fine with me. Though the more I thought about it, the more I realized there were feelings there, as I did have a crush on her, even still. Admittedly, there were still feelings there for Gunner too…

I quickly typed back:

>I work until 2am.

I looked up again, watching for my manager, making sure they didn't see me on my phone. It vibrated again.

>I'll be here :)

I shifted from one foot to the other, trying to reason with myself. Seeing Lita would probably be a better idea than seeing Gunner. If I was honest with myself, I knew that Gunner could get me out of my panties just as easily as Lita could. The cons of being a bisexual—both the male and female sexes have power over you.

I decided to be honest with her

>My ex is in town.

I waited a few seconds, sighing, as I hated myself. Then my phone vibrated again and I looked at the message, my eyes widening.

>Bring him too ;)

My whole body tensed, my sex clenching at the thought of not only having Lita all over me, but Gunner too. I mean, why not? All three of us were single, and what straight guy like Gunner would turn down a threesome with two hot women?

My hands shook a little as I typed.

>I'll see what I can do lol

***

I finished up work and headed back to my loft. When I pulled into my spot, Gunner was already outside of the building, having a cigarette. Again, he was sexy. I thought about Lita's words, which made my forehead break out into a sweat, my whole body tingling with anticipation.

I wiped above my lip and got out of the car. I walked up to him, my hands in the pockets of my leather jacket.

"Cher," he said, flicking the butt away from us.

"You still sucking on the cancer sticks, I see," I said.

"I'm stressed out," he said, shrugging a bit.

"Is that why you're here?"

"What do you mean?"

"I mean, the last time I saw you, we had an angry fuck, and then you left in the morning and that was the last I saw of you," I replied. "That was three years ago."

He nodded, putting his hands in the pockets of his jeans. "I know. It was sucky of me to do that. I was in a bad spot, though. You know that."

"But is that why you're here?"

"For a quick fuck?" he asked, unsure.

I nodded. "Yeah."

"Nah," he said, tossing his hair over his shoulder. "I really wanted to actually talk to you."

"About?"

"Was kinda hoping I could take you out to dinner," he said sheepishly, with a smirk.

"What if I had a better idea, something we could do tonight?" I asked carefully.

"Yeah?" he asked. "Like what?"

I stepped towards him, put my hands on his chest and stroked under his leather jacket. The scent from his cologne and the leather material filled my nose, making my sex clench again, empty, wanting. I wanted Gunner inside of me, mostly because he was familiar. I wasn't really into random hookups.

"I have a friend," I said, looking into his baby brown eyes.

His brow rose. "A friend? A girlfriend?"

I nodded with a little smirk. "A girlfriend, yeah. I'm supposed to go see her tonight. She mentioned bringing you along for the ride."

"What kind of see are we talking here?" he asked.

"Exactly what you're thinking," I said, looking at his chest. "The sexual kind."

"You want a threesome?" he asked, surprised.

"Well, I could go by myself—"

"No," he said, cutting me off. "I'm into it."

My heart began to race, and I turned from him, trying to play it cool. "Then let's go. Lita won't wait up all night."

***

It was another tense ride to Lita's. I stopped in front of her house once again, this time with Gunner sitting beside me in the passenger seat.

My heart drummed within me, making my stomach do a flip, as I thought about what I was going to do. It was on a whim, really. I had never experimented with ménage before. It was something I was obviously open to, but the chance had never come up before... until now, a hot June night.

"Here we are," I said finally, my mouth feeling dry.

"Nice digs," he said.

"Yeah," I said with a smirk. "Come on."

I got out of the car, Gunner following. Again I had my keys in my pocket and wallet with my phone in it on my wrist. I led the way up to the door.

I smoothed my bangs a bit and licked my lips, then pressed the doorbell. It was a tense five seconds before Lita opened the door, looking pretty fucking sexy in a silky black robe, her hair again up in a messy bun.

"Hey lover," she said. She grabbed my hand, pulling me towards her and kissing me passionately. She broke away from me and looked at Gunner. "Oh, yum!"

I laughed nervously, pointing. "This is Gunner. Gunner, this is Lita."

He nodded to her. "Hey."

"Come on in," she said, her hand still in mine.

Gunner walked in, closing the door behind him. Lita led me through to the living room once again.

"Drinks?" she asked, her eyes sparkling.

"What do you got?" Gunner asked.

"I think I have some Jack Daniels," she said coquettishly. "If you can handle it."

He laughed a little, nodding. "I can handle it."

"Really? What about me and Cher?" she asked. "Can you handle us too?"

He nodded again. "I know I can handle Cher."

"Maybe not," Lita said. "She was pretty freaky last night with me. But, fuck, was it good!"

"Then why not get to it?" Gunner asked. "Why the drinks?"

Lita smiled devilishly. "Oh, we can skip the drinks."

She pulled me into her, kissing me once again, her tongue and the stud in it wrapping around my own and her hands going to my face gently. I felt Gunner walk up right beside me, closing the distance. His scent filled my nose, mingling with Lita's perfume. He reached out, moving my face to him, claiming my mouth suddenly with a hot kiss as well.

It was that mix of the new and exciting with Lita, and the familiar and comfortable with Gunner, that made me wrap my arms around his neck, pulling him in deeper. I wanted both of them so badly.

Lita helped me take my jacket off, which she threw on the couch. She then took hold of my hips, kissing at my neck as I tilted my head back, still in Gunner's arms. Her hands went up to my breasts, her tongue moving over my skin as she massaged them. Gunner pushed his hips into mine, his erection pushing into me, making me gasp.

The heat rose from deep within me, a blush inking up my neck to my face and filling my cheeks. I felt feverish and sweaty with desire, my blood rushing through me, my heart thumping in my ears. I felt that ball in my stomach, a tight need—I wouldn't be satisfied without having them both.

Lita turned me towards her, kissing me once again, her lips soft, but not too much softer than Gunner's. It was just different, a different flavor. She pulled my white T-shirt up over my head, exposing my bare stomach and my bra. Gunner's hands moved to the straps, and he kissed at my neck as he pulled them down my arms. I reached behind me, undoing my bra and letting it to the floor.

Lita went straight for my chest, kissing the right breast and sucking on my nipple. Gunner turned me a little, so that he could do the same, taking in the left nipple into his mouth. I held onto them for dear life as I tossed my head, moaning loudly. The sensation of two mouths working their magic on me was almost too much.

Lita trailed kisses up my chest to my collarbone, while Gunner's hand moved down under the band of my jean shorts and slipped under my panties. His index finger brushed against my sex, making me tingle. A gush of wetness unleashed.

"Fuck," he said under his breath.

He pushed his middle finger into my folds, finding my clit and rubbing it slowly. I had to give it to Gunner that he still knew how to push that button and do it right. My legs began to shake as Lita kissed me, my mind running a mile a minute as I tried to hold on. But Gunner was good—too good. He kissed my bare shoulder as he rubbed my clit just the right way, sending me toppling overboard.

I held onto Lita as I pulled away from her, moaning loudly as my legs went almost completely to jelly. My whole body shook, and I tried to keep myself from crumpling to a pile on the floor from the orgasmic shudders.

Lita's hands went to my shorts, undoing them and slipping them off of me, my panties following. She then grabbed my and Gunner's hands and led us to the bedroom. She pushed me down on the bed, running her hands over my thighs, making me shake once more from an orgasmic pulse.

Gunner had his shirt off and was sitting on the end of the bed. Lita looked at him for a moment, smiling slyly before she crawled on the bed towards him. She got off the bed and stood before him before she sunk down to her knees.

I watched from the bed. Gunner's breathing picked up as she undid his jeans and pulled out his throbbing cock.

"Ooh, very nice," she purred. "You don't mind, do you Cher?"

I shook my head, my eyes eating up the sight.

"Good," she said, looking down at his cock.

She licked at the tip, making Gunner grunt a little. She then licked from the very base, up the shaft, swirling her tongue and the stud in her tongue around the head.

"Oh, fuck," he called out, his hands gripping the sheets on the bed.

She smiled once more before she took him into her mouth, going even deeper than I could ever. I wasn't really one for deepthroating, but Lita did it with a skill that amazed me... and turned me on all over again.

I got to my knees, crawled over to them and stroked Gunner's back and shoulders. As Lita went down on him, he leaned his head back, kissing me. We made out like we needed each other to breathe until he pulled away from me abruptly.

"Oh shit, I'm gonna come," he said.

Lita stopped, sitting up, just holding his cock gently in her hand. "Oh, not yet. I think you need to take turns fucking us first."

She stood, undid the belt on the silky robe, seductively pulled it off and discarded it at the bottom of the bed. She then walked over to the nightside table and pulled out two condoms. She kept one on the table, opening the other.

"I get to go first, as I am hostess," she said, nearly skipping over to Gunner.

He had kicked off his pants completely, and his hair was tied back with a hair tie. He let her put the condom on him, before she straddled him, putting his cock at her entrance and sinking down on him.

"Oooh, fuck," she said, tossing her head.

She began thrusting, as Gunner held onto her thighs. She got a good rhythm going, pursing her lips as she moaned loudly, her cheeks flaming brightly. She looked at me, licking her lips.

"Kiss me," she demanded.

I leaned forward, doing as she asked and kissing her passionately.

"Shit," Gunner breathed.

I didn't know how long Gunner was going to last. He wasn't a "hair trigger," but in all honesty, it was a hot situation and I wouldn't blame him for letting it go. But, surprisingly, he seemed to hang on, letting her ride him.

Lita suddenly sped up, going pretty rough and pulling away from me as she moaned loudly, her nails digging into Gunner's shoulders. She came pretty hard, only slowing when the intensity was obviously overtaking her, her thighs and arms shaking, her stomach quivering.

"Mmm," she said, before she let out a little giggle.

She gingerly stood from him. Gunner stood abruptly and pointed to the bed.

"Get on all fours, Cher," he said. "I have to fuck you, now."

I didn't need to be told twice. Lita handed him the new condom as he pulled off the old one. He put it on and got on the bed as I assumed the position. He lined himself up at my soaking entrance, pushing into me swiftly. I called out, as that little intense pulse overcame me from being filled up after so long.

Lita got on the bed before me and lay down in front of me, her legs spread on either side of me. I knew what I was to do—Gunner was going to fuck me, and I was going to eat her out.

As Gunner thrusted into me, I lowered my head down and spread her lips, licking up her juices before I headed right for her pierced clit. I flicked it a little, making her gasp, trying to concentrate on giving her what she needed as well as getting what I needed from Gunner. It was no easy task.

I licked at her clit, sucking it into my mouth. She bucked her hips into me a little, her hand going to my head, holding me in place. I could feel Gunner's sweet cock sliding in and out, hitting my G-spot perfectly from my ass being raised in the air, the arch in my back.

I moaned loudly as Gunner's hands held my hips firmly, pulling me into him as he thrust. I wasn't going to be able to hold out much longer. I knew Gunner was probably aching from it too, needing to spill over.

I clenched my muscles in my sex tight, which caused him to jolt a little, moaning in surprise. It was a shock to my system too, making the slow throbbing of the orgasm start to come at me in waves, building quickly.

I continued to lick Lita, who bit her bottom lip as she moaned, throwing her head back. Her thighs shook as the orgasm overtook her, but I didn't stop. I continued to suck on her clit, even as Gunner sped up, causing the orgasm to zip through me and come to a head, exploding within me.

I called out, pulling away from Lita as I slapped the mattress hard, grabbing a fistful of the sheets. Gunner slowed only slightly as he came, pumping into me as he filled the condom and letting out a low, guttural, animal-like moan.

He pulled out of me as Lita grabbed hold of me, holding me in her arms and cuddling me. Gunner disposed of the condom before getting on the bed and spooning up behind me. Our heavy breaths filled the room, our hot, sweaty bodies bound together. I fell asleep in utter bliss.

***

Gunner and I slipped out in the morning and went back to my place. It had been a hot night of multiple sessions with Lita, until we were all spent.

I lay in bed next to Gunner, who looked me in the eyes, as we were still awake, surprisingly.

"Are you and Lita dating?" he asked.

I shook my head. "Not to my knowledge. Why?"

"Because I miss you, Cher," he said quietly.

I swallowed hard, turning on my back. I looked up at the ceiling. "We broke up though."

"Because we were butting heads about music," he said. "I like to think that I've matured since then."

I smirked, looking at him. "So, you're admitting that you were the problem?"

He nodded. "I do, and I was the problem. I was letting my ego get ahold of me. Your band is amazing. You are amazing. That's why I miss you so much."

I smiled a little. "I guess no one else lives up to the Cher Swinton name, huh?"

He chuckled. "Nah. No way. Can I take you out to dinner?"

"Why don't we stay in?" I asked.

"We can do that too," he said. "What about Lita?"

"What about her?"

"Are you going to invite her as well?" he asked seriously.

"Do you want me to?"

He shook his head. "No. I want this to be you and me, Cher. I mean, last night was pretty epic, I'm not going to lie. But it made me realize that what I was thinking was right. We should try again."

If I was going to be honest with myself, I knew that Lita wasn't in the mindset for a relationship. In reality, I wasn't looking to date Lita, anyways. It was sort of fulfilling a high school fantasy. It was definitely exactly as I wanted it to be, maybe even better.

I looked into Gunner's blue eyes, smiling a little. "It was a blast, right?"

He chuckled again. "Yeah, it was."

"But you want it to be you and me, right?" I asked.

He nodded. "Yeah. I mean, every once in a while, if you want to invite Lita... I wouldn't say no."

"Of course not," I said with a smile. "So, second chances? Is that what all this was about?"

He grabbed my hips, pulling me into him. He let his nose rest against my cheek. "You know how I feel about you, Cher. Not that I'm crazy enough to turn down a threesome."

"Figured," I said with a laugh.

I heard my phone go off. It was Lita, once again.

>Thanks for the wild night, lover ;)

I smiled a little and typed back.

>No worries. We should do it again sometime.

>For sure.

I licked my bottom lip a little, knowing that what Lita and I had was special. It was a summer fling, but an epic one, no doubt.

I put the phone down on the side table before I turned back into Gunner, who had his eyes closed. I cuddled up into him, smiling to myself, my head on his chest. He stroked my arm before he kissed the top of my head, making me smile wider.

I guess it was a one-time thing, being a Midnight Queen.

The End

Flowers for Kate
Estelle Pettersen

Chapter One

Kate

London

It was 1988.

I was twenty-two, close to finishing my business degree at the University of London, and ready to step into the nineties, hoping for a better world. Irish band U2 was rocking it, Reagan was U.S. president, and the Berlin Wall divided Germany's east from west. Video had killed the radio star a decade earlier, and we adored films like *The Princess Bride*, *Dirty Dancing*, and *Wall Street*. As for fashion, it was big, wild, neon, and in-your-face.

Sitting at a booth at The Beat nightclub, I grinned at my best friend, Andy. He had dressed in a floral blouse, high-waisted jeans, and four-inch pumps. His face mimicked the flawless perfection of a French courtesan—powdered pale, blushed pink, and painted fuchsia on the lips.

"Ya bloody poofta," some dick sneered at Andy as he walked past us.

"Homophobe! What's your damage?" Andy shouted, flicking his shoulder-length blond hair.

I wrinkled my nose in disgust. "Ignore him. You're way better than that turd."

"That asshole is why I hate mainstream clubs." Andy rolled his eyes and groaned. "They're full of them."

"We won't stay for too long," I assured him, placing my nearly empty beer glass on the table. I readjusted my hoop earrings before shaking the neon bangles on both wrists—lots of bangles.

The club's speakers blared U2's haunting song, "With Or Without You." I felt desire running in my veins when I spotted the goddess, Isis, on the dance floor. She was a ripe slice of heaven in tight jeans, an off-shoulder T-shirt, and white high-top sneakers. The dark-haired angel danced with her friends in the most alluring manner, leaving me in a trance. Her slender body swayed in perfect sync to the song while the men dancing near her inched closer. She ignored them, closing her eyes and touching the curves of her sensuous hips.

Seduce me, I wanted to say to her.

Seduce me with your dance.

Seduce me with your body.

Seduce me with your eyes.

As if she heard me, her eyes fluttered open and gazed toward me. She slowed her dance almost to a halt and bewitched me with her soft stare. Her eyes, dark and hauntingly beautiful, sparkled with passion as her full lips curved up in a captivating smile. *Damn, you're all woman, and you're beautiful!* I grinned, showing my large front teeth. I felt as if someone had cast an Egyptian love spell on me, and I was spiraling over the edge, losing control.

"Hello? Earth to Kate." Andy waved his hand, distracting me from the honey-skinned goddess.

"Uh, yeah, I got a little carried away." I flicked my dark-blond hair away from my face, then rubbed my widened turquoise eyes.

"Carried away by what or whom?" Andy asked.

My eyes searched the dance floor, then scouted the neon-lit bar, only to find a sea of unfamiliar faces and, alas, no ebony-haired angel. My shoulders slumped as the anchor of disappointment sank in my heart. "I guess she was just a dream," I whispered despondently.

"Uh, say what?" Andy raised his eyebrows.

Ignoring Andy's question, I stood up. "Let's go to the rooftop bar. I saw Frankie take the elevator up there earlier tonight—she's with that American guy."

"Oh, meow!" Andy curled his slender fingers, clawed the air, and grinned. "Did I just hear a hint of jealousy in your voice?"

I narrowed my eyes at him. "She and I ended our relationship last year, and she can date anyone she wants. Besides, we're good friends now. My heart is intact."

"You, my dear, are always standing, even after the punches.

Remember the fight you put up with Professor Reece in our strategic management class?"

"Yeah, yeah, I know." I laughed softly, still eyeing the elevator. "C'mon. Let's go and say hello to Frankie and her man."

"Cool bananas." Andy stood up and adjusted his shiny, black heels. I wished I had a pair like those.

***

"Hey, lady." I hugged Frankie and kissed her cheek. She resembled a hot rock star with her long, wild mane, fishnet gloves, miniskirt, and thigh-high metallic boots. Her electric-blue eyeliner was thick and heavy against her obsidian eyes. On the other hand, her boyfriend was a classic preppy with his styled dark hair, polo shirt, designer jeans, and deck shoes. Frankie pulled herself away from me and wrapped her arms around him.

"Hey, Kate. Jasper and I are just chillin' tonight."

"Schweet!" I inhaled the fresh night air and sighed, admiring the beauty of the starlit sky that roofed us.

I tore my gaze from the sky and searched the open-air landscape, hoping to find the woman who'd caught my eye earlier. People swarmed around the outdoor bar like bees to honey while pop music enlivened the crowd, animated in dance and chatter. But nope, there was no sign of the dark-haired angel.

"Like, what part of America are you from?" Andy asked Jasper.

"Uh, Boston," Jasper answered, glancing at Andy's high heels.

"Ah. I've never been there," Andy said, shrugging his shoulders.

"Frankie and I plan to move to America one day." Jasper grinned, then kissed his girlfriend's forehead.

"*What?!*" My eyebrows shot up—if they could go any further, they'd have disappeared from my face.

"Yeah, we gotta talk," Frankie said curtly. She took my hand, and we marched toward the women's restroom.

Moments later, we stood face to face, arms folded, in front of the bathroom sink.

A woman behind Frankie pushed us to the wall. "Oi, you're blocking the mirror. Move!"

"Hey, bitch! Eat my shorts." I hoisted both middle fingers at the woman, then turned to Frankie. "Okay, what happened to the 'oh, I'm so independent' Frankie?" I pursed my lips. "You'd better talk, starting right now."

"I'm pregnant."

"Oh my God." My mouth was wide open, and my jaw slackened. "I'm going to have a spazz attack. Was it planned?"

"Nuh-uh. I just found out, but I'm keeping the baby."

"Do you love Jasper?" I asked.

"I do. I love him so much." Tears trickled down her face.

"Does he love you?"

"Yes. He loves me." Frankie wiped the tears from her cheeks and sniffed. "Shit, this whole baby thing is freaking me out. I'm scared."

"It's totally normal to be scared, but it's all good, yeah? I mean, you'll graduate before jet-setting off to Boston, right?"

"We're not moving to Boston. We're going to another city where Jasper's been offered a job as a geophysicist. And yes, I'll graduate first before I marry my Disney prince," Frankie said, hinting her usual light sarcasm.

"Will you wear a Disney wedding dress with the baby bump in tow?" I giggled, unfolding my arms.

"Oh, it's going to be deadly. I'm thinking of a minidress." Frankie laughed softly. "With the baby bump in tow."

"You'll look awesome." I stroked her shoulder gently. "Hey, can I ask you a favor?"

"Kate Calloway, you're one of my closest friends. What can I do for you?"

"Can I be your best woman at the wedding?"

Frankie grinned widely, showing off her white teeth against her olive skin. "You'd better be my best woman! I'll be careful about flowers, though, because of your pollen allergy."

"Ah, you know me and flowers. I panic when I'm in a flower shop." I winced at the thought of the itching, watery eyes, and nasal congestion.

"I need you, Kate," she said, biting her lip and tugging her skirt.

Feeling Frankie's uncertainty of her future, I pulled her in for a friendly hug. "Hey. I'm here for you whenever you need me."

If life were a book, Frankie's chapter as my lover had ended long ago. We were friends who delved into a relationship, but our passion was a delicate flower that wilted and died a slow death. Did I believe in true love? Honestly, no.

Right then, the beautiful woman who'd danced an enchanting spell earlier stepped into the restroom, eyeing me from head to toe. Her sweet smile poured warmth into my heart, filling it with passion. Letting go of Frankie, I smiled back at the raven-haired goddess. Whoever this woman was, she had become my new chapter in this book of life.

Chapter Two

Dahlia

Blimey! I found her!

I'd given up on finding the blond lass who caught my eye earlier, but here she was. Except she was hugging her lover tightly. Still, I couldn't help but smile at her—she was breathtaking.

"Hi," I managed to say, lost in her turquoise eyes. "I didn't mean to interrupt anything."

Removing her arms from her woman, she moved toward me and laughed softly. "It's not what you think. Frankie and I are just friends."

Frankie nodded in agreement. "Yeah, we go to university together."

"I'm Kate." She stretched her hand out, which I shook lightly.

"My name's Dahlia," I answered, my legs feeling like jelly. Would Kate walk away if she knew I had feelings for her? Emotions raced through my body, leaving my smiling mouth mute and my besotted eyes fixed on Kate.

"Hey, I'm just going to duck out and see how Jasper and Andy are doing," Frankie said, breaking the ice. She glanced at me and smiled before she left.

Kate nodded, then slowly angled her lean physique toward me. Oh, sweetness, she was stunning—the way her shoulders rolled and her hips swayed closer to mine. Her breasts rose as she breathed, alerting me of her erect nipples popping from beneath the soft cloth of her blouse. My heart pounded rapidly in response to the mouthwatering sight.

"I saw you earlier," she said.

"Oh yes, my friends and I felt like dancing tonight. We haven't had fun for so long." My cheeks were hot, flushed red from her attention.

"You can dance," Kate complimented as her eyes did a quick swipe up and down my body.

"Thank you, that's sweet of you." I glanced at her round breasts, her slender waist, then her shapely thighs and slender calves.

"I can barely dance," Kate said, her gaze lingering on my hips. "Maybe you can teach me sometime."

"I'd love to." I smiled, rubbing my hands together. "You look incredibly fit. I hope you don't mind me telling you that."

"I'm flattered," she replied, blushing red.

"Hey, I need to wash my hands. A man with sticky fingers grabbed them when he tried to dance with me. Only God knows what he did with his hands." I looked down at my sticky hands.

Kate wrinkled her nose in disgust. "Oh, that's so gross! God, you poor thing. It sounds like he was harassing you."

"Ugh, exactly. Do you know what he said to me? 'Baby, you look tasty. Do you want me?'" I laughed in disbelief as I washed my hands.

"In his dreams," Kate smirked, one hand on her hip.

"It'll stay in his dreams. I'm not into men."

"Oh!" Kate's eyes widened like saucers as if I'd dropped a bomb.

I took a paper towel from the dispenser and dried my hands before crumpling the used paper and tossing it into the trash. "Um, yes. Look—"

"Well, that makes two of us. I'm not into men either," Kate confessed, grinning from ear to ear.

I tilted my head and lowered my eyelashes as my lips curved into a sultry smile. I didn't have to say much, if anything at all, to show Kate that I wanted her. She mirrored me and touched my arm, caressing it as her lips touched my cheek.

"I'd rather be with you," she whispered into my ear, then planted a tender kiss on my jawline.

"I want you too," I rasped, feeling a euphoric high surge throughout my body. Daring to turn my face a little closer to hers, I kissed her nose. Then her right cheek. Then her lips. They were tender and luscious, sweetened by her cola-flavored lip gloss. I wasn't ready to take the soft kiss further as we had just met, so I broke away for a bit of space.

"You tease." Kate giggled, then bit her lip.

"Just wait," I hinted, taking the tease a step further. "Let's get some fresh air first."

Kate nodded, then clasped her soft hand into mine. She held my hand firmly and didn't let go. Emotions rushed to my head so fast that I'd forgotten my friends Megs and Stacey at the bar downstairs; they were chatting with some lads who played football, and I wasn't interested in talking with the men.

I didn't need to be with my friends, and I didn't want to leave Kate. She was an energetic force drawing me to a place where I wanted to be. A place where I could feel at home. Gazing into her eyes, I asked, "Can I be with you tonight?"

Kate's hand squeezed mine as her mouth formed the words, "Babe, you can hang out with me any time."

Not wanting to let go of her, I felt that it was time for her to take me *home*.

Chapter Three

Kate

I held Dahlia's warm hand as we weaved our way through the sea of partygoers dancing to The Bangles' "Walk Like An Egyptian" to get to my friends at the club. I was high with excitement, bursting with energy, and I couldn't wait to introduce her to them. My heart felt light as if it were a helium balloon in the bright blue sky. I only hoped that it wouldn't pop soon—or worse, burn from the sun's scorching heat like Icarus.

Andy, animated in conversation with Jasper and Frankie, spun around like a disco ball when I tapped his shoulder. "Ooh, nice top." He grinned at Dahlia as she tugged her peach off-shoulder T-shirt. "I'm Andy."

"I'm Dahlia." The tall beauty let go of her shirt to shake hands with my friends.

"Hey, Dahlia, I'm Jasper. It's good to meet you." Jasper released Frankie from his embrace to shake Dahlia's hand. "So, are you from London?"

"No, I'm from Southampton, but my family moved to London years ago."

"Really?" Frankie's eyes widened. "Southampton's not too far away from Bournemouth, where I grew up. What do you do?"

"Um, I sell flowers in Covent Garden."

"*No way!*" Frankie's jaw dropped.

I glanced at Andy, who raised his hand to cover a smirk. Silence attacked the air, icing our friendly conversation within seconds.

Dahlia folded her arms as her eyebrows knitted. "Did I say something wrong?"

"I'm allergic to flowers." I bit my lower lip.

Dahlia's eyes widened. "What kind of flowers?"

"Daisies, gerberas—and, uh, dahlias," I admitted, then touched her arm. "But I take antihistamines during the pollen season."

"Kate prefers kisses to flowers," Jasper teased, grinning at me. He had just saved my night and possibly my future love life.

Dahlia inched closer to me as I clasped her hand. "I prefer kisses too," she confessed.

"You two are so cute together," Andy cooed before turning to Frankie and Jasper to discuss Britain's unemployment rates, the lowest in seven years. He was a genius with an IQ of 160, and his mind was a bullet train that kept going.

"Dahlia," I murmured, "Is there anything you need? A drink? A smoke?"

"I'm a little hungry. Are you?" She stared at me, pleading to leave the club.

"Uh, yeah, I could eat," I mumbled. "Is there anything you fancy?"

Dahlia's dark eyes lit up as she licked her lips. "You. I want you."

"I'll just tell my friends that we're leaving," I responded, gesturing at Andy, Frankie, and Jasper.

Dahlia frowned when I released her hand, so I gently swept her long hair to one side, then snaked my bangled arm around her. "I'm glad I found you," I whispered, inhaling the sweet scent of lavender oil that fragranced her delicate neck.

I planted tender kisses on her jawline and rubbed the smooth curve of her hip as her hands found their way to the sensitive area just under my breasts. I had found the woman of my dreams, and she wanted me just as much as I wanted her. I didn't want to let go of her.

One hour later

"Blimey, this place is amazing! Is your friend rich?" Dahlia's eyes nearly popped out of her head at the sight of Andy's home. He had given me the keys to his place when I'd let him know that Dahlia and I were leaving. Andy was that kind of guy—a generous bloke.

"Andy's got royalty in his blood. His mum's a distant relative to the queen," I replied. "Plus, his dad's in the music business. He's an executive producer of some multi-award-winning record label."

"How posh," Dahlia murmured as her eyes glanced at the gleaming crystal chandeliers that hung above us in the marbled living room, decorated with large windows and vintage drapes. "This place is so familiar. I can't remember, but I feel as if I've been here."

I took her hand and led her to one of the guest bedrooms. "Come. Andy and company will be here any time soon."

"Company?"

"Yeah, Frankie and Jasper will probably crash here tonight. Andy usually has friends to keep him entertained in this big old place."

"It must be a lonely life for him." Dahlia toyed with a piece of her hair.

"Not really. He's got me." I grinned cheekily. "This place is like my second home. Ever since my parents kicked me out of home—"

"They kicked you out?"

My lips tightened as I stared at Dahlia. "Yep. They told me to bugger off and don't come back when they found out I was into girls."

She shook her head and frowned. "I'm so sorry to hear that."

"Don't be. I'm my own woman. I rent a tiny shoebox flat that Andy helped me to find."

"You're lucky you have each other."

"Yeah. We've been mates for a while."

After a momentary silence, Dahlia spoke softly. "Hey, I have an idea for the rest of the night. Let's make it about us. If we never see each other again, we'll always remember tonight."

I nodded and kissed her sweet neck. "I want tonight to be about us."

The guest room was dimly lit and cozy, with a four-poster bed, and an oil painting of an ancestor above the fireplace. Dahlia took small, graceful steps toward the oil painting and inspected every detail of the woman's portrait.

"That's Lady Margaret Forsythe. She's Andy's great-aunt or something like that," I commented.

She didn't respond and kept staring at the painting.

"Dahlia?" I tapped her shoulder to snap her out of her trance.

She slowly turned toward me as her skin glowed in the light from the decorative standing lamp. Her face wore pain as her large eyes shone with tears.

Wiping the tears away from her cheekbones, I asked, "Tell me what's going on?"

"The woman in the painting reminds me of someone I once knew and loved. I'm starting to remember my own past." Dahlia turned to me. "Can you promise me one thing?"

"It depends. What's the promise?"

"Learn to live and to let go of what you can't control."

"I promise you that."

"And for God's sake, Kate, please kiss me!"

"That I can definitely promise," I grinned, pulling Dahlia into me. Together, we fell on the soft mattress, where I landed on top of her soft and shapely body.

Brushing my lips against hers, I insistently deepened the kiss, probing through with my tongue. She took in the urgency of my passion and started ravishing me with delicious zest. The kiss we shared that night was neither timid nor tepid, but a scorching flame that could heat the ice-cold North Sea for eternity.

Chapter Four

Dahlia

"I want to make you mine." Kate thrust her hips into mine as I lay beneath her.

"You've got too many clothes on," I rasped as my fingers quickly undid her blouse buttons.

She grinned, shimmying her shoulders first, then removing the rest of her blouse. "Much better off?"

"Oh, much better!" I massaged her soft breasts with both hands, then licked each pink nipple. "You taste like strawberries."

"It's scented oil," Kate said while I inhaled and licked her skin's sweetness.

"Can I taste more of you?" I kissed each erect peak.

"Only if I can remove your top." Kate gently tugged my shirt.

I nodded, then allowed her to discard it, revealing my partial nudity.

"Is it hot in here?" I teased, getting rid of my jeans, panties, and socks.

"You're playing with me!" Kate giggled, taking off the rest of her clothes and unveiling her bare skin. She was beautiful.

Her body was an artist's masterpiece, and my hands begged to brush over her skin. Stretch marks ran along her curvy upper thighs intricately, creating reality in art with such detail. A bruise was detailed on her left hip, from bumping into a desk, she claimed. Her flaws enhanced her physical beauty. Blimey, Kate could have paved the way for impressionist artists to see the world through their own eyes rather than aim for perfect illusionism.

"Be my girl," I begged, searching her eyes for an answer as my hands stroked her inner thighs. "Be mine for tonight."

"I'll be yours for as long as you wish." Kate sighed, then kissed the crook of my neck, down to my right shoulder, and then my breast. "You're like magic that's hard to resist. Are you real, Dahlia?" I nodded my head, but when I looked into her eyes, she had them closed.

"Are you?" she repeated, opening her eyes and thrusting her pelvis into me.

"Yes," I moaned as her hand cupped my breast. Her mouth moved to my sensitive nipple, grazing it lightly with her teeth as if to tease. I let out a soft yelp.

"I won't hurt you," she promised, before her cherry lips engulfed the dark areola, sucking gently on the hardened tip.

"Oh, sweetness!" I exclaimed, arching my back. "Would you like to touch me?" I invited her to feel the most intimate part that made me a woman, guiding her hand there.

"Yes," she whispered as her hand accepted the invite.

"What do you want from me tonight?" I tucked a tendril of hair behind her ear.

"I want you to come for me." Kate's fingers rubbed my moist folds before exploring more of me. One finger slipped past my entrance, then two fingers, to feel my inner walls. The penetration rocketed my excitement, causing wetness to pool between my legs.

Closing my eyes, I felt every sensation of Kate's fingers expertly massaging my sensitive organ. She pushed further into me, applying more pressure as she increased the rhythm and speed of her thrusting fingers.

"You're going to make me come soon if you keep doing that," I said, rubbing her stiff nipples in circular motions.

"Don't come yet. I want to taste you first." Kate withdrew her fingers, coated with my scent, and licked them. I cried in frustration at the absence of her fingers in me, only to be promised, "I've got you. Trust me." She descended to my sex and rewarded it with a light kiss and teasing licks.

"Oh, what you're doing to me," I murmured, feeling the sexual tension rise high as Kate's tongue swirled and sucked my most sensitive parts. I began playing with my breasts, pinching my aroused nipples to heighten my senses.

"Come now," Kate commanded. "Let go."

Suddenly, I lost control, becoming undone as Kate's tongue repeatedly flicked across my wet folds, releasing a type of tension so strong that it burst into a powerful orgasm. "Oh, God!" I cried over and over again, feeling my body shake while her hands gripped my hips.

"That's it, Dahlia," Kate's husky voice encouraged as I released my own heat of ecstasy. "That's it. Feel it. Come for me."

Moments later, my body relaxed in pure bliss after the mind-blowing orgasm. Yet, I was emotionally energized—half a century could have passed, and I'd never felt so alive. I released my feelings in the sheer joy of lovemaking and thanked the mythological Fates that we met.

Turning on my stomach, I switched positions and climbed on top of Kate. "We're not finished. It's my turn to give back."

"What's the hurry?" Kate asked as I massaged her breasts. "We have tomorrow. And the day after."

"I want to give you something to remember from tonight." I planted light kisses on the side of her upper rib, then moved further down to kiss her hips.

"I don't want tonight to end." She stroked my head.

"We'll never forget tonight," I assured, kissing her neatly trimmed mound. I felt the softness of her fine pubic hair, which was different from a man's coarse and thick curls. Tracing my tongue over Kate's sensitive inner lips, I dipped it inside her entrance, causing her to moan. I looked up and stared at her feline turquoise eyes, intoxicated with desire.

"How does it feel, Kate?"

"It feels like heaven." Her hands stroked my hair, encouraging me to continue the foreplay.

"You're so wet," I murmured, lapping up her juices.

"Does it taste alright?" Kate asked. Her voice hitched with apprehension.

"It's delicious. Salty and tangy, yet addictive."

"What do you want, Dahlia?"

"I want more of you."

Kate's buttocks tightened as I squeezed them. My mouth descended on her sex again and released my tongue to snack on her. A whimper escaped from her lips, and she bucked as her butt cheeks clenched more.

"Don't stop!" Kate begged as she pushed my face further into her entrance.

My tongue, warm and silky, probed her sensitive flesh with ferocity and hunger.

"Keep doing that, and I'm not going to last," Kate moaned.

"Then come."

I nibbled and savored her clitoris, which triggered her to arch and cry out profanities that would make saints blush.

"*Dahlia!*" Kate hollered, gripping me tightly as every muscle in her body tensed before unleashing a flood of wet warmth into my mouth. She sighed several times, her rib cage rising and falling heavier and more rapidly before she finally let go.

"That felt so amazing," she whispered before drifting into sleep.

A bittersweet feeling attacked my heart as I watched Kate's eyes close to welcome sweet slumber. The released energy from our lovemaking had renewed my spirit. *It's soon time to leave,* a silent voice whispered in my heart. As old memories began to rush back, there was so much I wanted to tell her now. Yet, I couldn't. Not yet.

If only tomorrow would never come.

Chapter Five

Kate

Seven a.m., the next day

"This is Mark and Liz from BBC Radio One—"

Reacting to the morning assault on my ears, I reached for the snooze button and muted the radio. "Five more minutes," I whispered before dozing back to sleep.

"—and that was 'Wake Me Up Before You Go-Go' by Wham! We're predicting plenty of sunshine today, so take out your sunscreen and a hat. And next up is—"

I hit the button again to silence the darn alarm, only to be woken up five minutes later by Bananarama's "I Want You Back."

"Sod off," I cursed, rubbing sleep from my eyes. Andy didn't need a radio alarm clock in the guest room. Who knew why it was there?

"Hmm?" a sweet voice asked.

Turning my head to the right, I gazed at the beautiful dark-haired babe. Wide-eyed and gorgeous, she appeared almost innocent. *Almost.*

"Oh, I wasn't talking to you," I said as Dahlia smiled serenely. "It's the radio."

Dahlia combed her fingers through my tangled hair, handling it with gentle care. "You're beautiful, Kate."

I was about to switch the radio off as cheesy pop music wasn't my thing, but Dahlia's hand tapped my neon-bangled arm. Shit, I had forgotten to take those off in our frantic lovemaking.

"Don't. Leave the music on," she insisted. "Music brightens the mornings. Do you want to bathe with me?"

"Yes, please." I glanced at an elaborate wooden door across the room. Being a regular guest, I knew that a marbled bathtub waited for us behind that door.

Thirty minutes later, Dahlia and I came out of the bathroom feeling warm, clean, and fresh. The mid-sized towel showed off her deeply tanned legs, shapely calves, and the most perfect feet I'd ever seen. I didn't have a foot fetish, but she had gorgeous feet compared to my long, overgrown ones.

"Why are you staring at my feet?" Dahlia asked.

"Because they're perfect. Like you."

"Oh!" Soft laughter slipped from her pink lips.

"I enjoyed last night." I pulled Dahlia into me, kissed her forehead, then worked my lips to her cheeks and mouth.

I wanted to spend an eternity with Dahlia, yet she talked about living for the moment and enjoying what we had now. She had made no reference to the future. Something was in the air, and I couldn't pinpoint what it was, but it didn't feel good. It was as if I had eaten fairy floss that was too sweet, too perfect, but oh, so delicious. And I knew that I would somehow pay the price of feeling ill afterward.

Looking out the window, I saw a heavy fog. The swirls blanketed the English flower garden as if they were wisps of the fairy floss that would make me sick.

"Will you take a look at that?" I released Dahlia and pointed at the window. "We were supposed to get sunshine today, according to the weather report on the radio this morning."

Dahlia gazed at the swirls of thick mist that lashed against the glass. She shrugged her shoulders indifferently and walked to the bed to put her clothes on. I joined her in getting ready, asking for help to fix the buttons on my blouse.

"Sure," she replied flatly. Her eyes were downcast, and her face was stone-cold, absent of a smile. Joy didn't sparkle in her eyes today. That glimmer of hope had disappeared after last night.

"Dahlia, did I do or say something that offended you?" I asked. Was she upset with me? Or perhaps I read her wrong. I sometimes struggled to understand if someone was sad, angry, or indifferent.

Her eyes shot up at me. "No. You didn't do anything wrong. Everything was perfect."

"Too perfect?" I questioned.

"Perhaps." She sighed, then took my hand. "I see things that happen in the future sometimes."

"Are you a clairvoyant?" I raised my eyebrows.

"I don't know. My mother and my grandmother were able to dream or see things before they happened. I get that every now and then too."

"What do you see about us?"

"We will meet again. I also see you bringing me flowers." Dahlia chuckled, and the spark was back in her eyes. "Oh, and you'll be holding an artificial bouquet at Frankie and Jasper's wedding."

"Will they have their happily ever after?" I questioned.

Dahlia paused, then stared at me. "They will be happy together. At some point, Frankie will need to move on and focus on their children. Be there for her. Especially her daughter."

"What? I'm confused. I thought you said—"

"I've said enough." Dahlia let go of my hand and started walking toward the door. "Aren't you hungry, Kate?"

"Not particularly," I mumbled, but my stomach spoke the truth when it grumbled. "Okay, I may be a tad bit hungry."

"Come on, let's eat breakfast. I'm sure there's something in the kitchen."

***

"Did you hear Andy, Jasper, and Frankie come back last night?" I asked. It was a poor attempt to lighten the mood while eating cheap milk-soaked cereal and sipping expensive tea.

"I think I heard some voices," Dahlia answered, then leaned closer to me. "Do you want to know Andy's future?"

My lips curved upward into a slow smile. "Of course. Tell me. Will he become a famous artist or musician?"

"No."

"But he loves art, music, and all the things that make this world beautiful."

"Oh, stop with the clichés, honey!" Dahlia frowned. "Just because he appreciates music and art doesn't mean he'll be the next Picasso or Beethoven. You know your best friend."

"I see him in a relationship with a nice man."

"Try harder." Dahlia nudged my elbow softly. "He'll be married."

I cleared my throat. "But same-sex marriages aren't even legal in England."

"Not yet, but they will be legal here one day. There is always hope." Dahlia squeezed my hand as my heart soared with happiness. "Andy's true passion lies in politics, but you'll always have a friend in him."

Goosebumps spread across my arms. "Will I be in any trouble that I'll need him?"

"No, don't worry. Denmark is a great place to avoid the worst of the pollen season, by the way."

"Denmark?" *What the heck was Dahlia on about?*

"You'll see." Dahlia smiled enigmatically before devouring her breakfast.

We ate the rest of our meals in comfortable silence, with Dahlia's body ever so close, rubbing mine. Her body heat was a warm blanket on my soul, keeping me safe and snug. That was until I no longer felt it.

"Dahlia, do you think—" I lifted my head and turned to her, only to drop my jaw when I realized I was talking to thin air.

There was no Dahlia. The empty cereal bowl and the half-full cup of tea were still there, but how could someone made of flesh and blood just disappear? There was no science behind it. There was no logic.

How?

My eyes flooded with tears at the shock of Dahlia's vanishing act, and the burgeoning feeling of emptiness swamped my heart. That emptiness was painful. It was horrid and crippled with anxiety. I felt Wicked Anxiety's cold breath against my body, and her claws of despair and loneliness scratched at my shoulders. My chest tightened, and my stomach knotted with the fear of being alone.

The tears wouldn't stop. They just kept flowing as I hugged myself tightly, trying to maintain some control in a situation that lacked an explanation. *You are never alone.* I heard the voice of hope reason with my emotions. *Dahlia is always with you. Your friends are with you.* Right then, I heard footsteps coming from the hallway, along with human voices.

"They say that this is the new age of capitalism, but it's really a case of history repeating..." Andy rambled to Jasper and Frankie as they walked into the kitchen. "Hey, good morning, Kate. What—oh, fudge! Are you alright?"

"Oh, honey! What happened?" Frankie rushed over to me and placed her warm arms around my frail body, which shook with violent sobs.

"Dahlia wa-was right h-here seconds ago," I cried, pointing at her bowl and cup. "She just, she just..."

"Where is she?" Andy asked.

I turned to him, hugging Frankie tightly, and shook my head. "She's gone."

Chapter Six

Kate

"She didn't even say goodbye?" Andy leaned against the floor-to-ceiling bookcase.

"Nope." I crossed my arms and stared at a poster of The Cure on the wall above an antique radio. Andy's study was an eclectic mix of classic furniture and modern paraphernalia.

"Dahlia said that we would meet again and that I would bring her flowers," I declared. Three pairs of skeptical eyes met mine.

"I think she was telling porky pies." Frankie shook her head and rolled her eyes.

However, I didn't think Dahlia would lie.

Jasper leaned on the windowsill to gaze at the mist slowly disappearing outside while Frankie skimmed through today's news. She looked up from the page she read and frowned. "Guys, check out this article."

Andy tapped my hand, and we went over to Frankie, who spread the newspaper on the writing desk. Jasper moved away from the window and read the article over her shoulder. I squinted at the article, which Frankie read aloud:

Ghostly Encounter at London Nightclub

An eerie incident occurred at a London nightclub, The Beat, last night, when three female ghosts mingled with local clubgoers before vanishing into thin air.

"I had to deal with three terrified men after they danced and chatted with the spirits who then disappeared," the nightclub's manager, Sebastian Sharpe, said. "According to the men, the women were in their early twenties and didn't look or dress differently from anyone else. I reckon the ghosts just wanted to have a good time."

One of the men, Bruce Taylor, said, "Me and me mates were enjoying the night with these gorgeous lasses. Megs, Stacey, and Dahlia were their names. When Dahlia disappeared, her friends said she went to the loo. She never came back."

"We were going to ask if they wanted to look for their friend and come home with us for a cuppa, but they just vanished into nothing!"

When asked how he felt at that point, Bruce confessed, "I was so scared, I couldn't move. I'd never been so frightened in my life."

Sharpe said that the nightclub, on Russell Street, was an old murder site. "Last night marked the fiftieth anniversary of the night the women were brutally killed. They died on 18 May, 1938. Their names were Dahlia Thompson, Megan McLaren, and Anastasia Green," he revealed.

Frankie leaned back in the chair and chuckled. "It's interesting that the spirits were dressed for our time. Maybe they wanted to blend in and have fun? Well, they're cool. But—"

"Keep reading," I instructed. Frankie leaned forward and read the rest of the article.

Originally from Southampton and with Indian heritage from her mother's side, Dahlia was a dancer and flower seller who fell in love with Lady Margaret Forsythe. The lady bought flowers from Dahlia every week and invited her to the country manor when Lord Edward Forsythe traveled for business or visited his mistress.

Showing old newspaper clippings of the local gossip from the 1930s, Sharpe said, "Dahlia and Margaret had a love affair, only to be discovered by Edward when he returned home early. That was two days before Dahlia and her friends were attacked right here. The women were ambushed, sexually abused, beaten, and stabbed on this spot. Two died here, but Dahlia was found alive and taken to the hospital. She passed away later that night. The police never found the killers, but it was believed that Lord Forsythe was behind the murders."

When asked if the spirits had appeared at the club before, Sharpe replied, "No. This is the first time people have seen the ghosts. I occasionally hear noises when the club is empty during the day, but it's an old building, so I expect some creaks and slight movements of objects."

"*Blimey!*" I shouted Dahlia's favorite word. "Andy, tell us about your great-aunt Maggie—the one whose portrait is in the guest room."

Andy's red lips tightened as the color drained away from his gaunt cheeks. "She was my grandmother's older sister. Maggie chose to end her life during the second world war. Her husband, Edward, died of a heart attack shortly after, so my grandmother inherited this property."

Frankie drummed her fingers on the desk. "I'm all ears, Andy. Tell us more."

"Yeah, we're curious about the skeletons in your family's closet," Jasper drawled with his American twang.

Suddenly, a dusty crimson photo album fell from the bookcase, causing Jasper to move and Frankie to scream.

"Are you frightened, Kate?" Andy asked, nudging me while eyeing the tattered album.

"No." I frowned, annoyed at his assumption. "I've just lost a friend."

"And a lover," Frankie muttered under her breath.

Andy picked up the album and flipped through it carefully until he stopped about halfway. "Aha!"

"What did you find?" I moved closer to him and touched one of the album's delicate corners.

"There's something here for you," Andy said, gently rubbing the frail off-white paper inside the album. He then removed an envelope trapped between the pages and handed it to me. The envelope was marked with "Flowers for Kate" in delicate handwriting. I carefully removed the letter from the envelope to read it. The blue ink had faded, but the letter was easy to read, so I read it aloud for the others to hear.

18 May, 1940

Dearest Dahlia,

It's been two years since you passed away, and much has happened. We are in the midst of a terrible war—a second great war—and the only thought that gives me hope each day is of you.

The Germans have already invaded Denmark and Norway, but our prime minister assures us that our nation aims for victory despite the terror. I cannot handle more of living in fear. Edward is useless. He spends most of his time in Bath comforting his mistress, Yvonne, in these difficult times. My doctor encourages me to write letters as a way of dealing with my melancholy. I dream of us together, Dahlia, but I face the reality that you are nothing more than a memory when I wake up.

I live in hell because I live without you.

I escape the loneliness and isolation by remembering our dream of running away to America and starting afresh. That dream met its death on the day you closed your eyes forever. I will never forget the night you died in my arms at the hospital. You promised that you'd return to Forsythe Manor, but I didn't understand who Kate was when you whispered, "Kate will bring me back."

Those were the words that dominated your last short, wispy breaths before your eyes reflected the glassy coldness of death. I visited your sister afterward and asked if she knew anything about Kate. She explained your visions of the future before handing me a short note you'd written.

I must go now. Until we meet again. Perhaps in Valhalla. Or heaven. Or paradise.

Love always,

Your Maggie

Andy took the first page of the letter from me, then peered at the second one quizzically. The paper was shorter, thinner, and of worse quality. "Shall I read it?"

I nodded as he took the second page from my shaky hand. Clearing his throat, he began reciting the strange prose:

Flowers for Kate
In nineteen eighty-eight
Take my sweet soul
To where my Maggie lies.
Everyone pays a price.

What is your price, Kate?
A glimpse of love, only for it to disappear?
Take my sweet soul
To where my Maggie lies.
Do not wish for a dahlia
But for eternal love—
Such love neither wilts nor rots like the flowers.

"Andy, I think I've had enough," I whispered, as my shoulders slumped in despair.

Nobody spoke. My lungs couldn't contain a low whine, which made its way up my throat and escaped from my lips.

Agony shredded me.

I wept incessantly while Andy, Frankie, and Jasper held me together. I would never fully understand Dahlia, but I understood one thing now. I had taken her back to Maggie's home. *Their home.* In exchange, Dahlia had given me a gift—a glimpse of the deep emotional connection she had shared with Maggie. It sparked a new thought in my mind.

True love exists.

Chapter Seven

Kate

August 1989

I believed that Dahlia's spirit had been watching over me. Perhaps it was the gust of wind that blew behind me when I finished my final exams in June last year. Or the warm hand on my back during my graduation day—it was probably someone in the crowd who had accidentally touched me. Maybe I imagined things.

"Are you sure you want to do this again?" Andy's sky-blue eyes questioned mine as we walked in Covent Garden.

"That's why I'm here." I stopped and placed my hand on his shoulder. "I need closure."

"Well, if it's closure you need, then it's closure you'll get," he said, sticking his hands in the pockets of his corduroy slacks.

I had taken my antihistamine tablets, and we were on our way to buy flowers for Dahlia. It was amazing to see what the Forsythe money could buy. Andy had organized for a professional researcher to find Dahlia's grave. Her remains were carefully excavated and buried next to Andy's great-aunt Maggie, near Forsythe Manor. We gave Dahlia and Maggie eternal peace, visiting their graves with fresh flowers every month.

We celebrated Frankie and Jasper's post-graduation wedding at a local courthouse, and, as Dahlia had predicted, I held a bouquet of artificial flowers. The couple moved to the United States, where they had their baby boy shortly after.

Andy stopped strolling and glanced at a small shop ahead of us. "I think this flower shop is for you."

Its sign read *"Dahlia's Delights—we sell all flowers!"*

My mouth popped open as Andy grabbed my hand and marched inside the shop. The shopkeeper had her back turned, arranging a decadent bouquet of roses mixed with gerberas and lush greens.

I tapped my fingers on the counter to get her attention. "Excuse me, do you sell dahlias?"

She quickly turned around and smiled at Andy and me with her dark eyes and rose-pink lips. Her upturned nose and dimpled cheeks melted my heart.

"Yes, we have dahlias," the florist chirped. "The late summer is the best time to buy them."

I watched her ebony hair bounce as she moved her shoulders, leaning forward on the counter. I couldn't help but peer down her singlet, which revealed her full breasts. God, she was beautiful. Noticing my state of distraction, Andy nudged me. "We'll buy a bouquet of dahlias," he said.

The gorgeous woman glanced at me. "Would you like a card for the flowers too?"

Would I like a card? "Uh, sure."

I stared at the florist's voluptuous curves as she carefully handpicked the dahlias and arranged them into a stunning bouquet. She then searched through a stack of cards and plucked one out.

"Aha! I found the perfect card." She showed off her dimples, smiling widely as she gave me a card with a picture of a dahlia. *Was she flirting?*

Andy nudged me again, nodding to confirm that flirtation was in the air. Feeling light-headed and giddy, I couldn't help but giggle. I then cleared my throat and dropped my smile. "Sorry, I'm just a little nervous. You remind me of someone."

"Oh?" The florist raised her eyebrows.

"Her name was Dahlia."

"That's my great-aunt's name. She died tragically, according to my grandmother. My mum and I named this shop after her."

"Oh!" My eyes fluttered wide open.

"It's a sad story and a long one. I'm Laura." The florist gazed at me, then glanced at Andy.

"I'm Kathryn, but my friends call me Kate. This is my friend Andy," I said as he smiled.

"Uh, I'm just going to the bookstore next door. I'll be back in five." He winked, slipped his hands into his pockets, and walked out the door.

"Your boyfriend's cute," Laura quipped.

I wrinkled my nose. "Oh, no, no! We're not dating. He's my soul brother. I'm not into men, and he's not into women."

Laura's lips curved into a flirty grin, and she said boldly, "Good, because I'd like to take you out for coffee one day."

My eyes sparkled with delight as she handed me a neon-pink pen to write in the card—except she didn't quite let go as her fingers caressed mine. A burst of joy spread in my heart; it was as if Dahlia had led me here. "Learn to live and let go of what you can't control," she had said.

Gazing at Laura, I was ready to let go of the past. I wanted to feel love and let it lead me through this merry dance of life. As to what I wrote in the card, it would be my last message to Dahlia: "Thank you."

Thanksgiving Day, November 1999

"Vera Kathryn Richland, please stop blowing raspberries at Julian! Your godmother, Kate, and her partner, Laura, traveled all the way from Denmark to visit our home. They didn't come to see a circus!" Frankie scolded her daughter.

Vera stuck her tongue out at her brother when Frankie wasn't looking. The eight-year-old girl placed her forefinger against her lips and smiled wickedly at me. "Don't tell Mom," she mouthed.

Julian pressed his nose upward and snorted at his sister.

"Julian!" Frankie glared at her eldest child from across the dining table. "You're eleven years old, not five. Do that one more time, and it's off to your room!"

"Mom, it's not fair! How come Vee doesn't get time out?" The dark-haired boy crossed his arms and sulked.

I smiled and admired the freshly carved turkey surrounded by vegetable delights on the table. Turning to my true love, I whispered, "So, is it a 'yes' to having children?"

"Only with you." Laura planted a warm kiss on my lips.

"How's Andy these days? Is he enjoying life as a politician?" Frankie asked, passing me a bowl of creamy mashed potatoes.

I dumped a generous amount next to the juicy turkey slice and stuffing on my plate. "Andy's pushing hard in parliament to legalize same-sex marriages in England," I said.

"He and his partner, Daniel, are campaigning tirelessly," Laura added, then turned to me. "It's only a matter of time before it happens."

"Of course, they could always move to Denmark for a civil partnership, like we did," I suggested, pouring gravy on my meal.

"Denmark? Why Denmark?" Julian unfolded his arms and leaned forward.

"The company Kate works for expanded their business to Copenhagen, so we moved there," Laura explained.

"What's a civil partnership?" Vera asked, twirling one of her caramel-brown curls.

"A civil partnership is something that a government makes so girls who love girls or boys who love boys can get nearly the same rights as a married couple," I said. "Denmark was the first European country to do this."

"Well, I think that we should be able to marry whoever we want. Aaand everyone should have not nearly but exactly the same rights!" Vera exclaimed. She gave me two thumbs up and grinned, revealing a missing front milk tooth.

I grinned back, masking my pain, because someone was missing at the table, and he should have been here tonight. *Jasper Richland.* He'd died of cancer two years before, leaving Frankie a young widow with two fatherless children in Lester Harbor, far away from her family and friends in England. "Be there for her," Dahlia had pleaded with me eleven years ago. "Especially her daughter."

After dinner, we sat around the fireplace in the living room and relaxed with hot cocoa and chocolate chip cookies. "I'm blessed to have the best goddaughter in the world," I said to the girl.

"Yup!" She nodded up and down, then sideways, and up and down again. "I'm blessed to have the best godmother ever. Is it true that I'm named after you?"

"Well, your middle name is the same as my first name. I guess it's true."

Vera scooted closer and touched my shoulder gently. "Julian said Dad might come back as a ghost. Do you believe in ghosts?"

"No." I held her hand and smiled. "I believe in angels."

The End

About the authors

Alice Renaud

Alice lives in London, UK with her husband and son. By day she works full time as a compliance specialist for a pharmaceutical company. On Sundays she's a lay assistant in her local church. By night she writes fantasy and paranormal romance about shape-shifting mermen, lovelorn demons and thieving angels. A Merman's Choice is the first book in a trilogy inspired by the landscapes of Brittany (where she was raised) and Wales (her mother's homeland). She never completely grew up.

Callie Carmen

Callie started in the book business as a bookstore manager, which was the perfect place for her since she was an avid reader. After two years, she moved to the corporate office as a buyer and eventually became a senior book buyer. This was a rewarding career she loved.

Along the way, Callie decided to become a stay home mom, but couldn't give up working around books altogether. She volunteered to run the book fairs in her small town, six per year. At the same time, Callie started and ran A Child Oasis Company, with the sole purpose of placing a small book library in the homes of all the needy children in the nearby city.

As her children became teens, Callie found she needed more in her personal life than being the volunteer mom for the schools. She sat down at the computer one day and Patrick, Book One of the Risking Love series was born. Since then she has completed all six novels in the series. All can be read as standalone stories. She also wrote Dream Catcher, published by Black Velvet Seductions as part of the Mystic Desire anthology and a mobster romance, The Enemy I Know, in the Craving Loyalty Anthology. If you enjoyed reading James, find out more by reading Joseph and Anthony from the Risking Love series.

Callie is married to her soul mate and best friend. Like her characters, she is a firm believer in true love and love at first sight.

Gibby Campbell

Gibby is no stranger to the perils of romance. Single until the age of 37, she dated many an interesting (dare we say crazy) guy until meeting the love of her life, Jim. The two are now married and live in the Cleveland, Ohio area. They are joined by their very spoiled dog, Scoob. Gibby believes there is no true norm when it comes to relationships, and they all take hard work and dedication. When she isn't writing, she can usually be found hiking in the park or attending the theatre. Check out her blog at www.gibbycampbell.com.

Patricia Elliott

Patricia Elliott lives in beautiful British Columbia with her family. Now that her four kids are more independent, being 16+ years old, she has chosen to actively pursue her passion for the written word. When she was a youngster, she spent the majority of her time writing fanfiction and poetry to avoid the harsh reality of bullying. Writing allowed her to escape into another world, even if temporarily; a world in which she could be anyone or anything, even a mermaid. Dreams really can come true. If you believe it, you can achieve it!

Viola Russell

Viola Russell is the pseudonym for Susan Weaver Eble. A homegrown New Orleanian, she holds a doctorate in English Literature from Texas A & M University. She has travelled far and wide and relishes the memories she has made in places as distant as England, Ireland, Canada, and Jamaica and as near as Mississippi, Texas, Oklahoma, California, and Massachusetts. She lives with her husband Ben, the love of her life, in a New Orleans cottage and is most comfortable at her computer creating the worlds that drift into her imagination.

Estelle Pettersen

Estelle Pettersen is an Australian author and former journalist whose romance stories explore empowerment, freedom, and finding one's strength. She has a Bachelor of Arts degree, majoring in Journalism and Psychology, from the University of Queensland, Australia. Her second degree is an MBA from Queensland University of Technology, Australia. She is a member of Romance Writers of Australia and is passionate about history, languages, cultures, traveling, food, and wine. She is happily married and living in Norway these days.

More Black Velvet Seductions titles

The Brute and I by Suzanne Smith
Home by Keren Hughes
Only A Good Man Will Do by Dee S. Knight
Secret Santa by Keren Hughes
Killer Lies by Zia Westfield
A Merman's Choice by Alice Renaud
All She Ever Needed by Lora Logan
Nicolas by Callie Carmen
Paging Dr. Turov by Gibby Campbell
Out of the Ashes by Keren Hughes
A Thread of Sand by Alan Souter
Stolen Beauty by Piper St. James
Mystic Desire - Anthology
Killer Deceptions by Zia Westfield
Edgeplay by Annabel Allan
Music for a Merman by Alice Renaud
Joseph by Callie Carmen
Not You Again! by Patricia Elliott
The Unveiling of Amber by Viola Russell
Husband Material by Keren Hughes
Never Have I Ever by Julia McBryant
Hard Limits by Annabel Allan
Anthony by Callie Carmen
Paper Hearts by Keren Hughes
The King's Spy by L.J. Dare
More Than Words by Keren Hughes & Jodie Harrold
Lessons on Seduction by Estelle Pettersen
Rigged by Annabel Allan
Desire Me Again - Anthology
Mermaids Marry in Green by Alice Renaud
Holy Matchmaker by Nancy Golinski
Joshua by Callie Carmen

Whiskey Lullaby by Keren Hughes
Forgiveness by Starla Kaye
When the White Knight Falls by Virginia Wallace
Cowboy Desire – Anthology
The Bookshop by Simone Francis
Secret Love by F. Burn
Mischief and Secrets by Starla Kaye
Be Patient With My Love by Keren Hughes
Michael by Callie Carmen

Our back catalog is being released on Kindle Unlimited
You can find us on:
Twitter: BVSBooks
Facebook: Black Velvet Seductions
See our bookshelf on Amazon now! Search "BVS Black Velvet
Seductions Publishing Company"

Made in the USA
Middletown, DE
11 November 2021

52202871R00102